Grand Rapids, Michigan—a population of almost two hundred thousand—minus three thought Raine. When twelve-year-old Raine Evadeam moves to small town Nashville, Michigan to live with her great-aunt Adelaide in an old Victorian house, she quickly realizes there's more to her family than meets the eye.

Raine would be entering sixth grade at her fifth school district. Raine didn't make friends quickly or easily. Lucky for her, she was put in a class with two of her cousins—Cille and C.J. They shared a common interest of fighting bullies and were soon known as The Three Deams.

They grapple with a magical book, uncover family secrets, and take a journey on a road trip in Uncle Greg's semi-truck. Add ghosts and a lost puppy to their adventures, and what do you get? Find out in *The Evadeam Adventures,* a companion series to *The Trahe Chronicles.*

D1523953

THE THREE DEAMS
THE EVADEAM ADVENTURES
BOOK ONE

D.L. PRICE

COVER DESIGN & ARTWORK BY JERECO PRICE

To Jan,
Enjoy my new book!
—D.L. Price

A Story Tyme Realm LLC Trade Paperback Original

Copyright © 2015 by D.L. Price

Published in the United States of America.

Registered with Library of Congress
ISBN:13:978-1519147585
ISBN-10:1519147589

First Edition
Visit www.storytymerealm.com

ACKNOWLEDGMENTS

Gregg — Thank you for answering my constant phone calls and text messages. You shared great stories and invaluable information that helped develop this story. I appreciate it!

Michael — Thank you for reading this manuscript. My books were developed because of your support, patience, and love. You are wonderful and I love you very much!

Nicolas — Thank you for letting me forfeit some play time while I worked on this book. Someday, you will be big enough to read this and appreciate it. Love you, baby!

Jereco — Thank you for doing a fabulous job on the illustrations/ artwork design for my books and communications.

Diana and Ronald — To my parents, who raised three children including myself who had epilepsy and other ailments. You did a great job!

Cynthea Liu — Thank you for doing a fantastic job of editing my manuscript.

Spring Arbor writers' group — Thank you for listening to my readings and giving suggestions. Your inspiration is necessary for my writing career.

Family, friends and fans — Thank you for buying my books. Your feedback encourages me to continue writing.

God — Thank you, Creator!

DEDICATION
For Gregg and all the truck drivers of the world—you have jobs that I cannot do! You deliver things that the rest of us take for granted every day. I appreciate your hard work! Thank you!

THE THREE DEAMS

D.L. PRICE

WWW.STORYTYMEREALM.COM
WWW.DLPRICE.NET

CONTENTS

Raine

Grand Rapids, Michigan—a population of almost two hundred thousand—minus three, Raine thought as she stormed into her bedroom. Her dad just informed her that they were moving again. At twelve, she would be entering sixth grade at her fifth school district. She didn't make friends quickly or easily, and now she had to try to do it again. Her dad said with all their moving around "she had become a tough cookie". Sometimes too tough—she often made enemies with the school bullies. Her dad suggested that she sign up for a self-defense class to learn temper control and to not engage in unnecessary fighting. Raine was actually considering it until today when her dad made the moving announcement.

Raine's dad followed into her retro style

bedroom. Raine spun around with her arms crossed, "really, Dad?" she cried. "Why?"

Her dad explained that her mom had gotten laid off from her job, but she had found a great opportunity to be the caretaker of Raine's great-aunt.

"I can live anywhere within a couple hours of my Lansing office," he said.

"But why Nashville?" Raine asked. "Why the country? I love the city." Raine continued sputtering. "It isn't like we are moving to the cool town of Nashville Tennessee." She pointed at her country rock singer posters. "No, we have to move to small town USA in the middle of farm fields."

Dad sighed as he remembered when his wife had agreed that the small town would be a good place to raise their soon-to-be teenager. Plus, they would be closer to his Evadeam family and still in drivable distance to his wife's kin. He stretched to his full height—over six feet tall. He tried one more time to reason with Raine as he looked into the blue eyes of his only child. "This will be the last time. I promise."

Raine looked away. "I've heard that before." She watched as her dad's jaw twitched, which meant he was losing patience. She decided to back down. She plopped on her bed and tucked her short, dark blond hair behind her ears.

Her dad kneeled and put his hands on hers. "Raine, I promise. You have my word. As Brandon Scott Evadeam, I say that this will be the last move, at least until you graduate."

Even though the Evadeam word was serious, *sacred* even, Raine was skeptical. But deep down, she knew she had no choice anyway. "I am trusting you, Mr. President."

Her dad chuckled. He wasn't a president of anything, but he did work for the United States government. Raine knew that if it wasn't for her mom, Alexandria, they probably would have moved East years ago. Her dad's job took him to Washington a lot. In fact, he was hardly home. But her mother was not moving any farther from her family that lived in western Michigan.

Raine tried her best to accept their family's latest endeavor. She held back tears and made an effort to smile. "Okay, Dad. When do we need to start packing?"

Her dad stood. "That's my girl." After her father left her bedroom, Raine quietly let the tears flow as she wondered what the school would be like in Nashville, Michigan.

Animal Spirits

Months later, a large cat quietly walked the streets of small town Nashville. It was late August, but her black-and-white fur coat was already starting to thicken in preparation for cooler months. She loved the change of seasons on Earth—one of her favorite places in this world.

Cleopatra, otherwise known as Cleo to her human companions, was not of this universe. Her spirit had come from a much more complex realm. She was born from the Creator and given the job of a messenger—a guide. She had many missions throughout the worlds. Her current operation was simple. She needed to bring together three earthling children and her current caretaker, Adelaide Helldemueller. Thereafter, an apprentice would take over the job while Cleo continued on her own assignment with other Evadeam family members.

Cleo flicked her tail and watched a beam break through the atmosphere. Shimmering flashes of lights appeared when her messenger companion arrived.

A golden retriever dog trotted towards the cat. "Hello Cleopatra."

"Greetings Cherub" Cleo walked around the canine. "So why transform to a dog?"

"Don't kids like dogs?"

"Indeed they do."

"And aren't dog's fur thick?" As Cherub turned her nose upward, she continued "isn't it early for this cool weather?"

"Yes, but we are in Michigan," replied Cleo. "Do you know your mission?"

"I do. Raine is the human girl's name?"

"Yes." Cleo turned and started walking. "Come, we start right away." She meowed "If you must be a mutt, then, I do believe a puppy would be more attractive."

Cherub's body glimmered and for no human eye to see, she changed into a puppy. "Bark! Bark!"

"Try to keep up," Cleo meowed to her student. *Here we go,* Cleo thought breaking into a run.

Moving Day

As Raine traveled in a moving truck with her dad, she looked through the passenger window noticing a cat and a puppy run across the sidewalk. Without warning, they turned and ran right in front of their truck. "Look out, Dad!" she yelled.

Her dad swerved and hit the curb. "Whoa!" They came to a stop. "That was close," he said.

Raine let out a sigh. They had missed the animals who disappeared behind a brick building with two signs in front. One for an ice cream shop and another for a karate school. *Odd combination* Raine thought.

Refocusing ahead, Raine watched her mom's SUV turn out of view. The moving truck Raine was in was towing their smaller car as they continued to roll through town.

"Don't blink, Raine," Dad said. "If you do,

you might miss Main Street."

"Terrific," she replied glumly.

Boom! A loud noise echoed as their automobile lurched, then shook.

Dad glanced at the side mirror as he pulled over. "Ugh, the tire. I'll be right back." He unfastened his seat belt and hopped out of the cab. Within a few minutes he was back. "Yeah, it's a blowout, all right. I won't be able to change it with a full load. I'll need a tow truck with a big jack." He pulled a cell phone from his shirt pocket. "I should probably call Uncle Greg too let him know we'll be late."

Raine slumped in her seat. She was tired of riding. As her father made his calls outside, Raine thought of the Evadeam family. It was huge. Some of her relatives were supposed to meet them at their new house to help unload. Raine wondered how many people would show up. She rarely saw them, except for holiday functions. Though their moving here would be a big deal to them. *The more the merrier*, she thought. *Less work for me to do.*

It wasn't long before Raine saw Uncle Greg pull up in his oversized truck. As he climbed out, his lean body stretched over six feet tall like Raine's dad. But that was the only similarities. Raine noticed how different he looked from her own father. The Evadeams were an extensive mix of German,

Dutch, Irish, English, and French Canadian. There was also a rumor that they might be part—French Creole or American Indian. No one knew for sure, but some of the family members had jet black hair, tan skin all year long, and dark brown eyes. Raine and her dad didn't inherit those features, but her Uncle Greg had.

Raine's dad was one of seven children—himself, Uncle Coby, Uncle Larry, Uncle Greg, Uncle Ronald, Aunt Tricia, and Aunt Rhonda. Everyone called her dad Scott because there were so many other people named Brandon in the family. His father was named Ovid Evadeam and his mother, Adeline, passed away years ago.

"Come on, Raine," her dad beckoned from outside. "Get out and say hello."

Raine opened her door just as the tow truck arrived. Raine's dad explained this tow truck was equipped with a forty-ton bottle jack which could change a flat tire on a fully loaded moving truck. As the tow truck maneuvered into place, two kids jumped out of Uncle Greg's vehicle.

These were her cousins, C.J and Cille. C.J. the son of Uncle Greg, was just a few months younger than Raine. He was a little shorter and skinnier than her. He wore glasses, and most of his dark brown curly hair was covered by a Detroit Tigers baseball cap. C.J. and his three brothers were being raised solely by Uncle Greg. The boys' ages ranged from five to eleven with C.J. being the oldest.

"Cool hat," Raine said.

C.J. smiled. "Thanks."

"Welcome to Nashville," said Cille, the daughter of Uncle Coby and an only child like Raine. Cille wore her long sandy blond hair in two braids. She had big brown eyes and tanned skin. Cille was one of Raine's cousins who had epilepsy. The other was Diana who was younger than all of them. "Guess what?" Cille asked excitedly. "My mom and your dad pulled some strings. All three of us will be in the same class this school year. Isn't that great?"

"Yeah, yippy-skippy," Raine replied sarcastically. "So looking forward to starting a new school in the cow field." The moment Raine said the words, she regretted it. She could tell Cille's feelings were hurt by the look in her eyes. But before she could apologize, Cille turned to walk away. "Welcome anyway," Cille mumbled as she went back to her uncle's truck.

Raine called after her. "Wait, Cille—"

"Jeez," C.J. interrupted, "we know you don't want to move here. You didn't have to be mean about it." He followed Cille.

Raine sighed. "Well, this is off to a good start."

Helldemueller House

Soon, Raine arrived in front of her new home where her grandfather Ovid's sister, Adelaide Helldemueller, lived. Stepping out of the truck, she eyed the huge Victorian house. It was painted a beige-gold color with red, green, and white trim. Raine was told that it was one of the few enormous homes still standing in the historic downtown area of Nashville. Great-aunt Adelaide was recovering from a recent fall, and Raine's mom would take care of her in exchange for rent. "It's perfect," Grandpa Ovid had said when the announcement was made over a month ago. "My son's family is destined to live in the Helldemueller House."

Raine's mother came out the front door and started giving unpacking orders. Raine grabbed a small box of her favorite belongings from the back of the truck and headed up the porch steps. The rest of the family followed.

The large porch wrapped around the front of the house, welcoming newcomers. As Raine stepped onto its creaky wooden boards, her black-and-lime tennis shoes looked almost space-age compared to the old material used to build the house. Raine entered through the double front doors and found herself in a large foyer.

The foyer divided a parlor and a library; each room had a turret as the ceiling. Her dad had described the details of the house to Raine on the drive. The main floor had a kitchen, butler pantry, dining room, half bathroom, a bedroom with an adjacent full bathroom, and a living room facing the backyard. There was also an unfinished basement with a laundry room.

Raine admired the beautiful wooden staircase leading up to another level. An elderly lady with a cane, wearing a light yellow pantsuit, walked into the foyer.

The woman smiled and pointed her cane upward. "Raine, you and your parents' bedrooms are on the second level."

Raine eyed the petite gray-haired lady cautiously. She had a pointed Irish nose and big brown eyes that softened as she reached out to Raine. "Nice to see you again Raine. Why don't you help me up the stairs?"

"Aunt Adelaide, we can show them around," Uncle Greg said as he walked in behind Raine. "You shouldn't climb the stairs."

"Poppycock!" Aunt Adelaide responded. "I am healthy as a horse. Just have a little limp is all."

Uncle Greg laughed. "So why do you need a live-in caretaker?"

She was just about to say, *I don't*, but she stopped herself. Adelaide remembered that the girl needed to be here. As she turned to head upstairs, C.J. walked in carrying a large box.

He accidentally dropped it to the floor. "Sorry," he said, wincing. "Hope there wasn't anything breakable in there."

Raine read the black writing on the box. *Raine's clothes – bedroom.* She shrugged. "No, just my clothes."

"No wonder it was so heavy," C.J. said.

Raine smiled and thanked C.J. for helping. Cille walked in behind C.J., followed by Raine's parents and more family members. "Sorry for earlier," Raine said to Cille.

"It's okay."

"Friends?"

"Still friends," Cille said with a smile.

Aunt Adelaide waived the two children to follow her and Raine. "Let the adults move the heavy boxes. You can help unpack and carry the empty boxes into the basement."

They followed up the stairs. "Now just call me Aunt Adelaide, children. Great-aunt Adelaide Helldemueller is quite a mouthful."

As Raine helped the aunt up the wooden steps, she noticed the stairwell was filled with family portraits. An old black-and-white picture beckoned to her. Raine brushed a cobweb aside as she looked closer. It had many people in it, including a large cat that sat right in front.

Aunt Adelaide pointed to a pretty young woman standing behind the cat. "That is me in my younger years."

"You were very beautiful," said Raine. "I mean, you still are."

Aunt Adelaide laughed. "Yes, I was known to be a looker in my day."

"Come on, Raine," called C.J. from the top of the stairs. "Cille and I have your bedroom picked out for you."

They brought her to a front bedroom that overlooked a street. Cille stood beside Raine at the window. "We figured you would miss the city noise, so we put you in the bedroom closest to the side road. Plus, this window is great for watching sunsets."

"*And* if you have any overnight guests," C.J. added, "they can sleep in the spare bedroom across the hall. But here's the best part. Your parents' bedroom is all the way over on the other side of the house."

Raine smiled. "You have this all figured out, huh? And who do you suppose those guests will be?"

C.J.'s returned the smile. "Why, us, of course!"

"Yeah," agreed Cille.

"C.J. and Cille," Aunt Adelaide said, "tell Raine all about our grand adventures in this house." She winked then left the room.

Raine's cousins filled Raine with stories about their past summer visiting Aunt Adelaide. They had spent many days exploring the creepy, cobwebbed attic filled with Helldemueller family artifacts. C.J. hinted that they hoped Raine would want to join them as they continued their explorations.

Then, C.J. and Cille led Raine out of the room, and Raine was shown the rest of the house. After the tour, Raine decided that the century-old home might not be such a bad place to live after all.

After a long day of unpacking, Raine's dad ordered pizza for dinner. The family ate and talked. Aunt Adelaide explained that the house had always been owned by a Helldemueller. She married into the Helldemueller family—a prominent local family.

She now was one of the few remaining. After dinner, Aunt Adelaide asked the children to carry her tea tray to the parlor. As they walked down the hallway, she pointed out family members in the pictures that filled the walls.

Raine entered the parlor and almost tripped over a black-and-white cat lying on the floor. Cille helped Raine balance the tea tray and place it on a tea cart. Raine looked down at the cat. "Where did you come from?" She didn't realize her aunt had any pets. The cat purred and rubbed against the children's legs.

"Oh, Cleo comes and goes as she pleases," explained Aunt Adelaide. "She must have come back to welcome you."

Raine bent down and petted Cleo. She noticed that the cat resembled the one that they had almost hit in town. In fact, the cat also looked a lot like the one in the old photograph. *How odd*, Raine thought.

The cat meowed. A green stone dangled from her collar. "Wow, that is pretty," said Raine as she touched the stone. Raine looked up and noticed a green stone on her aunt's necklace too. She stood and gestured toward her aunt. "The jewel on your necklace matches Cleo's." Raine watched in wonderment as her aunt's stone started to glow. Raine looked down at the cat and watched as the collar stone also gave off a soft green glow. *Weird.*

"So they do," Aunt Adelaide said, and then the glowing stopped. Their conversation was interrupted by Uncle Greg announcing they were leaving. Good byes were said with promises that Cille and C.J. would be back soon.

An hour after the additional family members left, Raine's mom declared it was bed time. Raine was tired, but she could not get her mind off the glowing stones. As if reading her thoughts, Aunt Adelaide touched the necklace pendant. "Head for bed, dear. We will have another day for answers and stories."

Even though she was curious about the green stones, Raine nodded in agreement. She was very tired. As she climbed the stairs, she remembered the way her aunt climbed earlier which made Raine wonder if she truly needed a caretaker. Raine was going to try her best to not like the great aunt too much. After all, the old lady was partly to blame for their move. Plus, Raine was always cautious about getting too attached to anyone since her family never seemed to stay in one place for long.

But her dad did promise they wouldn't move again. Not this time.

Family Secrets

After a few weeks in the Helldemueller House, Raine became comfortable with her new home and had grown fond of her great aunt. However, she was having difficulties at her new school. It wasn't long before Aunt Adelaide noticed. One early Saturday morning in October, the two were sipping tea in the parlor. She had been keeping her aunt company while her parents went into the nearest big town to grocery shop. Raine had volunteered to stay behind to make breakfast tea for Aunt Adelaide. Even though Raine wasn't much of a tea drinker before she moved, now she found herself enjoying it.

As the two sat on a set of antique wingback chairs, Aunt Adelaide noticed Raine's right foot moving back and forth rapidly. "You seem nervous," Aunt Adelaide observed as she stirred the tea with a spoon in her rose-patterned cup. "Is something wrong?"

Raine hesitated at first, but she had grown to trust Aunt Adelaide. There was something she wanted to get off her chest, and Aunt Adelaide seemed like the right person to confide in. She was an incredibly good listener.

"I'm really not fitting in at school," Raine explained. "And I've already made at least one enemy."

Aunt Adelaide tilted her head in thought. "Ah." She knew Raine had confronted a bully at school who had been picking on the little kids, but she had thought perhaps the issue had gone away. Apparently, it had not. She placed a hand upon Raine's. "Perhaps a good prayer before you get on the bus would help."

Raine sighed. She had been hoping for better advice.

Then Aunt Adelaide added, "Remember, Raine, that boy is mean for a reason. He probably doesn't have a wonderful great-aunt like me."

Raine smiled.

"Maybe you should invite him over here sometime," Aunt Adelaide said. "What was his name again?"

"Gideon, and no, I won't invite him over."

"Then perhaps you should just try being nicer to him." Aunt Adelaide advised. "One should act as one wishes others to act toward them."

Raine sighed again.

Aunt Adelaide paused. "This isn't helping, is it?"

Raine shook her head.

"Oh, dear. Let me think." Aunt Adelaide snapped her fingers. "Then we shall concentrate on your nervousness. I will just have to send one of my angels with you. They are good for soothing the nerves and protecting you from all bad vibes."

"Angels?"

"Yes, angels, or guardians, as they are sometimes called." She leaned toward Raine and whispered, "Did you know our family has many guardians?"

She is having a senior moment thought Raine as she shook her head.

"Would you like to hear the story about how it all started?"

"How what started?"

"How our families became one and were assigned guardians."

Raine was now convinced her aunt was being silly, but a good story would help pass the time away. "Sure" as she eyed the breakfast platter.

"It all started with the Evadeam

Enchantment and the Helldemueller Hex." Adelaide took a sip of her tea and continued. "Well, the Evadeam family possesses special gifts—talents. And the Helldemueller family were given a hex to try to break the Evadeams' powers."

"What?" Raine leaned forward. "What powers?"

"Let me explain the history first and then I'll tell you all about that."

Raine raised an eyebrow. Sometimes Aunt Adelaide could be a bit too mysterious.

"The Evadeams and the Helldemuellers were bitter enemies for hundreds of years."

"But aren't you an Evadeam who married a Helldemueller?" Raine pointed out.

"Indeed, I am." She took a sip of tea. "Until I met Peter, God rest his soul." She lifted a small plate of breakfast pastries from a wooden tea cart. "Doughnut?"

Raine took one and anxiously waited for the rest of the story.

"Now where was I?" Aunt Adelaide said.

"The two families were enemies."

"Oh, yes." She laughed. "Peter and I did cause a ruckus in our day. Peter's family threatened to disinherit him if he married me."

"So what happened?"

Aunt Adelaide glanced toward the front

entryway, with a faraway look in her eye. "One day, while we were all in this very parlor, arguing about our situation, someone knocked on the door. Mr. Helldemueller—Peter's father—answered it. He brought in a very tall, black man who walked with a cane. I will never forget the freckles on his face. He called himself Hachmoni, an unusual name. He said he had a gift for Mr. Helldemueller. The gift was to be handed down through generations to come." Aunt Adelaide's eyes held Raine's gaze. "It was a book."

"A book?"

"Yes, a very large book that was titled *The Prophecies and Powers of Trahe.*"

"I've heard of that book from Dad. It's like our family bible or something. Isn't it?"

"Yes, dear. Very good!"

"So what does this book have to do with your marriage to Peter?"

"The book was magical," Aunt Adelaide said seriously. She wiped her hands on a floral napkin. "The moment that book was handed to Mr. Helldemueller, everything changed. Or maybe it was the cat who changed everything."

"Cat?" Raine wondered if this cat was the same one she had seen in the photo.

"Yes, it was the cat. After Hachmoni said his farewell, he left a black-and-white cat behind.

Funny how none of us noticed the animal come in with the man. But there was a big cat sitting right in the middle of the parlor after Hachmoni left. Mr. and Mrs. Helldemueller tried to catch up to Hachmoni, but he was nowhere to be found. And believe me, they tried to find him. It was like he disappeared into thin air, then left a cat."

"Wait." *Was Aunt Adelaide's pet, the same cat as the one left behind?* Raine thought. That made no sense. Cleo would have to be a zillion years old. "Do you mean *your* cat?" Raine stared at the black-and-white animal that was sitting by the window.

"Yes, my Cleo. She stayed even after Peter passed on." She leaned forward again and whispered, "At times I overheard him speaking to that feline creature. I thought my husband was getting delusional in his later years. I swore I heard him talk back to himself."

"So Cleo is very old."

Aunt Adelaide grinned. "Yes, as I. But I have known cats to live many years past their owner's life."

Raine looked at Cleo in disbelief. "She doesn't look that old, and how can a cat fix a family feud?"

"Magic."

Raine rolled her eyes and took another bite of her chocolate sprinkled doughnut.

"Sometimes, believing is seeing. Would you like to see the book?"

"*You* have it?"

"Well, of course I do! Let's go to the attic."

"Are you sure you want to go all that way?" Raine said as she helped her great aunt up from her chair.

"Exercise never hurt anyone," Aunt Adelaide said. "Only *lack* of exercise does!"

The two of them climbed the stairs to the dark and dusty attic. Her cousins had talked about their attic adventures, but this was Raine's first time in it. Raine slowly opened the creaky, wooden door. She spotted an old, dusty red velvet rocking chair in a corner by the window. "Here, Aunt Adelaide, sit down." She helped her into the rocker.

Aunt Adelaide pointed toward the door. "Turn on that light switch."

Raine spotted the switch behind a coat rack. She flipped it on, making the room seem a lot less spooky.

"Now look for an old luggage trunk."

Finding the trunk was not as easy as Raine thought it would be. The attic was filled with all kinds of stuff. There was old furniture, crates, containers and even toys. After a few moments of searching among Aunt Adelaide's things, Raine found it. It was next to a wooden rocking horse. She pushed the rocking toy away to get to the trunk and felt a chill in the air. Rubbing her shoulders, she tried to ignore the eerie feeling that crept up. She focused on the old wooden trunk. "It's locked."

"As it should be," replied Aunt Adelaide, "and I have the key." She pulled a golden chain from her pocket. The chain was identical to the necklace Aunt Adelaide wore around her neck. They both had gold key pendants, and in the middle of the keys' faces were the green stones that matched Cleo's collar. Aunt Adelaide handed the chain to Raine. "Try this key."

Raine was so excited to have the key in her hand. She wished Cille and C.J. were here. They would love this. She went back to the trunk, held her breath, and inserted the key. *Click*. She gently pushed up the heavy trunk lid. Dust flew everywhere, making her sneeze. Once the dust cleared, she stared into the trunk.

"Well?" said Aunt Adelaide.

"The trunk is filled to the top. Looks like a bunch of old clothes."

"Never mind all that. Get to the bottom."

Raine heard Aunt Adelaide get up and walk over. "Be gentle with everything. Some of it is very old."

Raine pulled out all kinds of stuff including clothes, books, and envelopes she assumed were filled with letters. She piled it carefully on the floor. Finally, Raine came to the last item—an old gold mirror. It had painted roses decorating the handle and the back of the mirror. Aunt Adelaide touched it as if she was remembering something fondly.

"It's pretty," Raine said. "I think you should keep it in your bedroom."

"I think I shall. I could use it, and it would look nice on my dresser."

Raine looked back down into the trunk. "So where's the book?" she asked staring at the empty chest.

Aunt Adelaide leaned on her cane. "Patience, dear. Now this is the tricky part. Gently peel back that corner of the liner."

Raine followed instructions. She pulled on the chest's fabric liner and revealed a key hole underneath.

"Take the same key and unlock it."

Raine inserted the key and gave it a turn. A secret compartment opened. Raine's heart pumped faster. Inside was a huge leather-bound book. She pulled it out. "Why is this hidden?" she asked.

"Now this is the part of the story you've been waiting for—because it's magical," her great-aunt replied.

Magical Book

"So what is magical about the book?" asked Raine as she felt the leather cover.

Aunt Adelaide took the book from Raine, returned to her chair, and placed it on her lap. Raine sat at her feet. "This book holds our family history. As you turn the pages, our family history unfolds. You will even see updates, even though the book has been locked up for years in the trunk. That is one of the reasons it's magical. No one has physically written in the book as far I know. Not even me."

Raine was skeptical. "What do you mean? Words just magically appear on the pages?"

Aunt Adelaide clapped her hands excitedly. "Yes, and the most curious part is that it seems to predict the future, too."

Raine was not believing her great-aunt. "Can

I see? Open the book."

Aunt Adelaide smiled, "What is the magic word?"

"Please?"

And the book opened, but not from magic. Aunt Adelaide carefully turned the pages, revealing black lettering and pictures. She stopped at a page far in the back of the book. "Yes, it's doing it again."

Raine stretched and looked at the open page. She was staring at a drawing of herself kneeling next to Aunt Adelaide. The image of herself and Aunt Adelaide appeared to be reading a book!

"No way!" Raine jumped up in disbelief. "How did it do that?"

Aunt Adelaide shut the book. "I told you. *Magic.*"

Raine rubbed her sweaty palms on her jeans. "Man, I wish Cille and C.J. were here."

Aunt Adelaide smiled softly. "Let's bring this book downstairs. Then, you can call on that fancy cell phone of yours and invite them over." She handed Raine the book. "I want you to read this."

"Why?" Raine backed away and pointed at the book. "It is haunted."

"No, Raine. This book is protected by angelic powers. It explains about our protectors and our family enchantments." Aunt Adelaide facial expression and voice soften "Do not be afraid. This book was left to our family as a guide, to help those who can't help themselves."

"To those who can't help themselves," Raine repeated. "You think it could tell me how I can fix my situation with Gideon?"

"Perhaps."

Raine eyed the book.

"Magic" whispered the great aunt. "But nothing to be afraid of. We can say the protection prayer and you can wear this."

Aunt Adelaide held out the chain with the key. "It possess magical qualities. It helps protects those who wear it. And you'll need it to lock away the book."

"Really?"

Aunt Adelaide nodded her head and gently placed the necklace into Raine's hands.

Raine took the necklace and slowly put it on. She was hesitate to wear something that might have magical powers. Then, she looked down at the pendant hanging from her neck. It was so beautiful. The stone started to glow, and she heard a meow. Startled, she glanced at the attic door to see Cleo walking in. The cat rubbed against Raine's legs. Raine picked up Cleo and stroked her fur. She glanced down at the pendant again. "Are you sure you don't want this back?"

Aunt Adelaide shook her head. "Keep it. It's

a gift, just take good care of it. When you leave the house, you should lock the book back up."

Raine set Cleo down and gave her great-aunt a big hug. "Thank you." *The stones illuminated.*

"Let's call my cousins." Raine helped put everything back in the trunk, and they made their way to Raine's bedroom.

Aunt Adelaide sat on the girl's bed as Raine called and made arrangements. To Raine's delight, her parents arranged to pick up her two cousins on the way back from their errands. Then, Aunt Adelaide left Raine with her thoughts and settled in for a morning nap

Alone, Raine touched the pendant, knowing it had to be valuable and possibly dangerous. The sound of the wind howling outside drew her attention to the window. It was beginning to snow lightly. It would be a good day to do some reading.

She sat on her bed and studied the book more closely. The title *The Prophecies and Powers of Trahe* was embossed in green lettering across the front. Though she wanted to wait until Cille and C.J. arrived, she knew she had to take a peek again. She flipped to the back hoping to find the image of Aunt Adelaide and herself again, but oddly the pages in the back were blank!

Why? Maybe Aunt Adelaide would know. She would have to ask her later.

Then, she flipped to the beginning of the book to see what was there. The first pages covered the history of the Evadeam and Helldemueller family dating back over one hundred years. Raine flipped through more pages filled with writings until something caught her eye. The book fell open to a hand-drawn picture of the parlor in this very house. There was a man resembling great uncle Helldemueller talking to another man described as Hachmoni. Hiding under a wingback chair was a cat. This was the moment that her great-aunt had talked about. The moment that changed everything.

She ran her fingers over the picture. *"Cleo."*

Raine flipped through page after page, looking for anything else that she might recognize. Before long, she heard the sound of a car pulling up in the driveway. C.J. and Cille had arrived. Raine raced downstairs, but didn't get a chance to mention the book.

Her parents handed bags to the kids. "Bring the grocery sacks into the kitchen. Your mom will put the food away," ordered Dad.

After helping, the kids sprinted upstairs. Raine told them everything and showed them the book.

C.J. plopped down on Raine's bed with the book in his lap. "I can't believe Aunt Adelaide showed you this. I wonder why she didn't share it with us first?"

Strange thought Raine.

"So where do we begin?" C.J. said.

Cille and Raine sat on either side of him. "Duh, at the beginning," replied Cille.

C.J. made a face. "It's not a regular book though. Maybe we start at the end *Lucille*."

Cille groaned at her birth name. Lucille Evadeam inherited her grandmother's namesake. *Why do parents punish us?* she wondered. One thing the Evadeam family did right was nickname those who were named after other people in the family. Lucille didn't have too many nickname options— Lucy, Cille or Cil. "Now you are being silly, Coby James," drawled Cille.

Raine laughed as Cille used C.J.'s real name.

"Or do we start at the middle *Lorraine*?" asked C.J. sarcastically as he used Raine's full first name. He randomly opened up a page.

"We should start from the beginning," Raine remarked ignoring her cousin's name reference. "Otherwise, we'll miss something and we won't understand what's going on in the middle."

The three cousins settled down. They studied the family trees of the Helldemueller and Evadeam families. "Isn't that odd that both families are in the book?" Raine commented. "Especially since they did not unite until after Aunt Adelaide married

Peter Helldemueller? How come the book goes backward even though Mr. Helldemueller had the book before his son was married?"

"Yeah, that is strange," said Cille.

Raine's mom yelled up the stairs that it was time for lunch. Cille put the book on the bed. Before they headed downstairs, Raine picked the book back up. She wondered if her dad knew about it.

As the kids sat down at the kitchen table, Aunt Adelaide walked in whispering to Raine's dad. Raine noticed that they looked at her and then the book in her lap. *Did her dad already know about the possible magic in their new home?*

"Hi, Aunt Adelaide. Are you rested?" asked Cille.

"Yes, indeed. Thank you."

Raine decided to take a chance and placed the book on the table. "Dad have you ever." Before she got a chance to finish the sentence, her dad grabbed the book.

"We don't want to spill anything on this." He glanced over at his wife whose back was turned. "I'll go put it in the parlor." Raine watched as Cleo followed her dad. She also noticed that her dad changed the topic during lunch, so the book was never brought up. After they ate, he followed the kids and aunt into the parlor. "Your mom isn't very fond of this book, so let's keep it away from her. Okay?"

"Okay," replied Raine but she thought it was odd to keep the book a secret from her mom. Unless, the book scared her mom. Raine pushed the book away and Cille picked it up.

"Cleo and I'll sit with the kids. Why don't you go see if Alexandria needs any help cleaning up the kitchen," suggested Aunt Adelaide. Her nephew hesitated, but then thought it best to make sure his wife stayed out of the parlor momentarily.

After he left, C.J. peered over Cille's shoulders. "Where's the good stuff, like the stories about aliens and talking cats?"

"Aliens?" Cille whispered examining the book.

"Yeah. I heard that Grandpa Ovid Evadeam was once abducted by aliens."

Raine rolled her eyes and looked over Cille to study the book. "There is no such thing as aliens." She sat cross legged on the plush rug in front of the fireplace. "I do have a question, Aunt Adelaide." She reached over and turned to the page that had the hand-drawn picture of the parlor with the cat under the chair. "How did this get in the book? Isn't this the scene that you told me about? Where Hachmoni gave you the book?"

Aunt Adelaide leaned in. Her eyes scanned

the page. "Yes, that is that very same day. Hachmoni is just how I remembered him to be."

"So who drew this picture?" asked C.J. "Great Uncle Helldemueller? You?"

Aunt Adelaide laughed. "No, not me dear." She said with a smile, "That is part of the magic."

Raine groaned. She was not getting anywhere, yet she was excited to go through the book even though it left her with unanswered questions.

Cille thumbed through the book. "Oh, look at this!" She flipped to a picture of a unicorn. Then the next page had a unicorn with wings. "Is that a Pegasus?"

"There is no such thing as a Pegasus," said C.J. "This book seems to be pure fantasy."

"But it has our family tree and history in it," said Cille.

"Maybe Great-great Uncle Helldemueller drew these fantasy pictures when he went senile," explained Raine, "and Aunt Adelaide just doesn't know he did that."

"But I thought you said you saw yourself in this book," C.J. replied. "How do you explain that one? Unless you made it up."

Aunt Adelaide leaned forward on her cane. "So you are not believers, Raine and C.J.?"

"Not of mystical creatures. No." *But I can't*

explain the mysterious drawings, Raine thought.

"Me either," declared C.J.

"And you, Cille?" asked Aunt Adelaide.

Cille shrugged. "I don't know. Do you believe in this magic stuff? Maybe the drawings are magic but what they're showing isn't always real." She kept flipping through the pages. "Guys, look at this picture!" She pointed at the book.

Everyone took a look at the page. There was a picture of Grandpa Ovid and their cousins—Brooke, Jereco, Brandon and Diana. They were sitting in something that looked like an airplane cockpit. On the opposite page, the four relatives climbed out of a spaceship, fighting a large snake.

"It can't be them," whispered Raine.

"Of course, it is not really them," said C.J. "I just saw Brandon and Jereco last weekend."

"Maybe it's their future!" exclaimed Cille.

"No way!" Raine waved her hands across the book. "They're going to go off and fight a large snake? The drawing in the book itself doesn't make sense. Maybe Cille is right. Maybe some of the drawings are made up. This book was given to you years ago. It has been in the attic in a locked trunk, right? How is it possible that pictures of our cousins got into the book?"

C.J. scowled at the book. "Maybe someone is playing a joke on us"

"I don't know," Raine said as she stared at the picture of her cousins. It was drawn in the same style she had seen the drawing of herself with Aunt Adelaide reading the book, and that was real. "My dad knows about the book and doesn't want mom to see it. Maybe he would know more."

"He will tell you what I have already said. The book was left to our family as a guide. To help those who can't help themselves," paused Aunt Adelaide. "It's magical."

Just then, Cleo hopped into Cille's lap. Cille scratched behind Cleo's ears. "Grandpa Ovid always says that, too," Cille said.

"Says what?" asked Raine.

"Help those who can't help themselves," Cille repeated.

"Yes, my brother has a way with words," admitted Aunt Adelaide.

Raine stared at Cleo. "And how on Earth do we explain a cat who lives *this* long? Cleo has identical markings to the cat in the wall picture and the cat in this book."

No one answered.

"I guess we just have to read the book," C.J. said.

Raine's dad walked in. "Someone said something about reading a book?" He glanced at *The Prophecies and Powers of Trahe*. He sighed, "I guess

I was about your age when I first read this book. It is powerful, so please only read in our presence."

Raine noticed that her dad glanced at the necklace she now wore. "What about mom?"

"She is busy cleaning. Getting the house ready for Halloween decorations. Hey, how about if we go to the pumpkin patch tomorrow?"

"Can Cille and C.J. go?"

"Of course, they can." He walked over and sat in one of the chairs. Leaning over and picking up the book, he asked "So are you three ready for an adventure?"

"Yeah!" The girls chimed.

"Unless, this is a joke," said C.J. as he looked at his uncle.

Uncle Scott's face grew serious. "This is no joke, C.J."

Aunt Adelaide took the book from her nephew. "This book is magic—special." She paused, "The book seems to resurface when it is time."

"Then let's do it!" C.J. said brightly. "Let's read the book. If our cousins are going to fight snakes—real or fake—I still want to know what happens next."

Aunt Adelaide stood up. "Read the book, and it will come." She headed out of the room followed by the cat.

The Three Deams

The three kids spent the rest of the evening reading the book. The possibility of magic kept them interested for a while, but C.J. was the first to fade. "It is just a family tree book with some fantasy drawings in it."

Cille was the most engrossed in the book. "I think it's fascinating."

"I mean it's cool and all!" C.J. said. "But family members are travelling in spaceships and stuff—this has to be fantasy."

C.J. rubbed his eyes and walked over to the bedroom window. "Look, it's stopped snowing."

Raine peered over C.J.'s shoulder. "I would hope so. I am not ready for snow yet." She got up. "I'm hungry. Let's take a break."

"I agree," C.J. headed for the door. "Let's

pick this up again later."

Raine paused at the door. "Coming, Cille?"

"Yeah." Cille hesitantly put down the book. She traced her forefinger over the book title. A chill went up her spine. She shuddered and ran after her cousins.

That evening, after her cousins were asleep, Cille wrote in her journal.

Today, we were given a book to read — The Prophecies and Powers of Trahe. I not only read about our heritage, but also about grand adventures that our ancestors had. Hopefully, we'll have quests of our own. Great adventures that will take us to the unknown.

The following day, the kids enjoyed the pumpkin patch with hayrides, eating hot doughnuts and cold apple cider. It was a sunny, chilly day ending with pumpkin carving. They never got a chance to open the book again that Sunday before they were tucked in for the night at their own homes.

Monday came fast, and the three cousins could not wait to break for recess during school. They headed outside to their favorite spot—a bench located by the swings. What little snow that had fallen over the weekend had already melted, but it was still chilly outside. Fortunately, Raine wore her warm black winter coat and camouflage boots with green laces.

"Aren't you cold, C.J.?" Cille shuddered under her pink coat. Her blond braids stuck out of her matching winter cap. She pointed toward C.J.'s sneakers. "Where are your boots?"

"They don't come out until there is a least two inches of snow," he replied as he walked over to an empty swing and sat in it. "Oh, no. We got trouble coming."

The girls turned to see Gideon and his buddies with him.

Gideon was a bully. Cille's mom had said that they should try to be nice to him because his home life isn't the greatest. Cille felt sorry for Gideon until he was mean to the younger kids.

The stocky brown hair boy walked right past the girls and up to C.J. "You're swinging like a girl. Here let me help you." Gideon grabbed the swing chains from behind and pushed the swing as hard as he could.

"Knock it off, Gideon," said C.J.

"Cut it out," Raine said.

Gideon stared straight at her. "You want me to stop? Okay." He grabbed the chains, which whipped the swing to an abrupt stop. Gideon pushed C.J. on his back, hard. C.J fell face first into the ground.

Raine and Cille jumped off the bench and

ran up to him. "You okay?" Cille said.

C.J. pushed himself up. "Yeah."

"Are you sure?" asked Raine. "I see blood."

"Your lip is bleeding." Cille brushed bark chips from C.J.'s face.

"Oh, what's a little blood?" said Gideon. "Cry baby."

Raine tapped him on the shoulder. "What's a little blood?" As Gideon turned toward Raine, she punched him square on the left cheek. A crowd of kids had begun to gather. Some of them stared at Gideon with their mouths open. Someone whispered. "Gideon just got punched by a girl!" Gideon's face reddened.

Before Gideon got to his feet, the recess lady was there breaking it up.

Cille watched as C.J., Raine and Gideon left with the recess lady to go to the principal's office.

C.J. received a cold compress for his lip. He had an option to go home, but toughed it out when his lip stopped bleeding. His dad was called and gave approval that he could ride the bus home if C.J. wanted.

Raine and Gideon both received a three-day suspension for throwing punches. They spent the rest of the day sitting in separate offices until they were released to catch their buses home. Gideon walked by the three cousins at the bus loading zone.

"Watch your back, C.J." Gideon sneered.

"Don't worry about him," assured Raine.

Raine led the way onto the bus. The cousins were welcomed by applause and hollering from other kids. "Finally, someone told Gideon off!" a kid said. Then the chant began. "*Three Deams! Three Deams! Three Deams!*" until the bus driver shouted at everyone to settle down.

That is how the three Evadeam children were given a new name to call themselves. And it stuck.

Zero Tolerance

The rest of October went by with no incidentals at school. The kids avoided Gideon as much as possible. Out of school, they enjoyed the autumn festivities until the Evadeam grown-ups started talking in whispers.

Raine was realizing that their very large and eccentric family truly does have strange things happen to them. The most recent event was a suspected UFO sighting at Uncle Ronald's farmland. But later, authorities said only a small plane had crashed on the property. Not long after, however, family members disappeared. But the media said the members had been on a charter plane to the Bahamas, and it vanished within the Bermuda Triangle. A search team was still looking for them.

One November weekend, the kids approached Aunt Adelaide. "We are hearing all kinds of stuff," said Raine. "What's really going on with our family?"

The great-aunt looked tired as she sat in her favorite parlor chair. She spoke quietly "It is true. Some of our kin have vanished. Cleo, my brother, your cousins — Brooke, Jereco, Brandon and Diana — are part of a rescue mission."

"A cat and kids?" asked C.J. skeptical.

Raine thought all these stories sounded crazy like something out of tabloid magazine.

Aunt Adelaide pointed to the book on a coffee table, "answers you seek are in there."

Raine picked it up. She turned to the page that they had mulled over several times. The drawing of Grandpa Ovid and their cousins. They were sitting in an airplane cockpit. She glanced to the other picture, the one where the relatives were climbing out of a spaceship. Raine had an overwhelming feeling of dread. For a moment, she believed. "How can we help them?"

"My dear Raine, believe and pray," said the great-aunt as she squeezed the young girl's hand.

Cille put her hands on the book. "We need to study it. Not just read it."

The Three Deams quietly agreed. The rest of November, they spent much of their free time reading the printed heirloom for any clues to the disappearances of their family members. They had no luck figuring out how to help them. "If it is even true," reminded C.J.

Meanwhile, their school peers, were always approaching The Three Deams about the news story. The three cousins didn't know what to say other than what was already in the news.

Then, one December afternoon, an incident changed everything for The Three Deams. It was a beautiful, sunny, wintery Michigan day and the principal decided to let the children out for one more afternoon recess. Raine thought it was too cold to hang outside, but the younger students were thrilled. They could play, make snowmen, and throw snowballs if they were being careful about it. The older kids, however, were too cool to play and too *cold* from sitting and standing around. Raine and Cille sat on their favorite bench while C.J. jumped up and down to stay warm.

"You know," Cille said to C.J., "if you wore boots, gloves, hat, and a warmer coat, you wouldn't be so cold."

C.J. scowled at the constant reminder. "Okay, *Mom*."

Cille smiled back and turned her attention to the playground. "Uh-oh." Gideon and his posse were ganging up on a couple of little boys.

Raine glanced in the same direction.

"Gideon!" She got up.

"Don't do it, Raine," said Cille. "You can't afford anymore detentions or suspensions. Plus, it's almost Christmas break."

Raine sat back down on her hands. She gritted her teeth as she watched Gideon. She wasn't like that for long though. She was off the moment she heard one of the younger kids cry and noticed one was C.J.'s brother.

"Gideon stop it!" ordered Raine.

Gideon stopped when Raine approached him. "Oh, it is one of the members of the alien family."

Raine ignored his comment and stepped in between Gideon and the boy. "Go to C.J." The sibling nodded and ran towards his brother. The other little kids took cue and ran off too.

"Gideon, you should know better than to bully one of my younger cousins. Why don't you pick on someone your own age?"

"Okay," said Gideon as he stepped forward forcing Raine backwards. Raine proceeded to step back and tripped over something. Gideon took advantage of the situation and kicked her.

Meanwhile, Cille noticed her younger cousin heading their way. C.J. ran forward and over his shoulder yelled, "Where are the playground monitors?"

She pointed at the opposite end of the yard. "Over there. I'll go get them."

"Wait!" C.J. said, "Raine needs our help!" He instructed his brother to find a recess lady.

Cille saw Raine was on the ground trying to get up with Gideon kicking her. Cille and C.J. raced to their cousin's aid. Together, they knocked Gideon down so they could help Raine up.

Minutes later, the Three Deams and Gideon were in the main office, waiting for their turn with the principal. Cille went first into his office. She was nervous. She had never been in trouble at school before. She explained everything to Principal Pfent.

"The school has a zero tolerance rule," explained the principal. "Three-days suspension."

"What?! I'd never been suspended before— not even detention," cried Cille.

He went on. "I will make sure to explain the entire situation to your parents when they come to pick you up."

Gee. Thanks.

C.J. was next. He came out of the office telling Cille he got the same speech. "Good luck," said C.J. to Raine.

Raine nodded and waited her turn after Gideon. She stared at her lime green laces that threaded through her army boots. The office clock struck three. It wasn't the first time she had sat in the office, awaiting sentencing. She kicked her boot at the brown carpet as she sat on her hands to keep herself from a nervous habit of cracking her knuckles. She wanted to be calm, but she couldn't help but think about how her parents would react to the news that she was in trouble again. Her mom would definitely be upset, but she worried more about her dad. Brandon Scott Evadeam he had been working round the clock to help with the investigation of the disappearance of his family members. This would be the last thing he'd want to be dealing with right now.

Click. The sound of Principal Pfent's door opening made Raine look up. Her gaze met Gideon's as he stepped out. Gideon smirked at her. He opened his mouth to say something, but he was interrupted by a man's deep voice—Gideon's dad.

Raine averted her gaze. "Raine?" Principal Pfent called from his office. "Come in." She quickly entered the principal's office. She knew Gideon would be in trouble with his father and didn't want to hang around for that. Even though Raine didn't like Gideon, a small part of her felt sorry for him. Raine sank into the leather chair across from Pfent.

"So Lorraine ... " Principal Pfent paused, "Raine, I understand that you are having interpersonal issues with Gideon." He paused.

"And I'm also aware that your family is going through a lot now based on the news reports. Does that have anything to do with what is going on with Gideon?"

Raine shifted uncomfortably as her thoughts wandered to her family and the mysterious book. Raine's gaze met Principal Pfent's. "The fight was not about my family." She brushed her bangs out of her eyes. "Gideon was bullying younger kids again including my cousin." Raine sat up straighter as she told her side of the story. "I was just minding my own business on the bench when I saw him go after them. I tried to ignore the situation and let the recess ladies handle it, but they weren't nearby. So … " Raine spread out her hands. "I had no choice. He was acting stupid."

"We do not call people that, Raine. So how did Gideon get a bruised eye?"

"He pushed me down and kicked me. So I had every right to punch him back."

"*Raine*," Principal Pfent warned. "You know the rules. No fighting." He sighed. "I'll have to suspend you for the next three days. One more suspension and you could be kicked out from this school."

Raine frowned.

"And as you may know, C.J. and Cille are on suspension as well."

"But you shouldn't suspend them. They were just trying to protect me. They didn't mean to fight."

"They know the rules."

Raine gave him a dirty look. "That isn't fair."

"Zero tolerance, Raine, means zero tolerance." He stood up. "Suspension for everyone. Since winter break is only a few days away, you won't be returning to school until after break is over."

Wait a second, Raine thought. Maybe this isn't so bad after all.

"Your parents have been notified."

When Raine walked out of the principal's office, she didn't say much to Cille and C.J. when she collapsed into a hard chair. "Sorry" was all she could manage.

C.J. smiled. "I've decided to look on the bright side. We get three extra days off for winter break."

"It's not funny to me," Cille said. "I've never been in trouble before." She looked like she was going to cry. Raine tried to comfort her but it was no use, so she just picked at a black thread on her shirt and waited for their parents to arrive.

But only one parent showed up—C.J.'s dad.

Chocolate Shake Punishment

C.J.'s dad quickly walked into the school. He stopped in front of them "So, the Three Deams in trouble."

Raine couldn't look him in the eye. "Where's my dad?" she said meekly.

"He's on business as usual." Uncle Greg glanced at the office. "Wait here for a minute." Greg walked into the office to talk to the principal. A few minutes later, he came out. "Got all your stuff?"

The kids nodded.

"Come on then."

The kids quietly followed him out to the parking lot to a blue truck with an extended cab. C.J. took the front seat while Raine and Cille sat in the back. Greg drove in silence for a while until he pulled up to a small local diner that was known for cherry sodas and chocolate shakes. "Let's get some shakes."

Shakes? Raine thought. Shouldn't they be lectured over the suspension right now?

"Maybe hot chocolate would be better," Cille said, pulling her coat tighter before she hopped out of the truck.

"Agreed," said her uncle.

They settled into a corner booth. Raine spoke up. "So why are we here? Aren't you supposed to punish us or something?"

C.J. noticed a plate of food being carried over to another table. "Can I order French fries, Dad?"

"No," Greg replied. "You'll ruin your appetite for dinner."

"Won't the hot chocolates do that anyway though?" Raine questioned.

Cille kicked Raine under the table.

Raine grabbed her leg. "Ouch!"

Uncle Greg smiled. "You're right." He waived over the waitress. "An order of French fries, please." He looked at the kids. "What would you like to order?"

"A cherry soda?" asked Raine forfeiting the hot cocoa.

"And a chocolate shake for me," piped up C.J. The rest of them ordered.

"Sure thing, Greg." said the waitress. She returned shortly with their drinks.

Cille gently blew at her hot chocolate to cool it.

"So Dad … " C.J. glanced around the restaurant. "What's our punishment?"

Greg sipped from his mug. "Well, son, it is up to Raine's and Cille's parents to decide for them." He lowered his voice. "Personally, I don't think I would have done anything different if I had been in your shoes. I'm glad you tried to help your cousin and brother." He leaned back into the black leather booth, and his voice suddenly sounded more formal, parent-like. "That said, you used aggression to retaliate against aggression. You need to find a better way to handle this type of situation at school."

Raine harrumphed.

"C.J.," Uncle Greg continued, "I will find extra chores for you to do."

"Oh, man!" C.J. slumped in his seat.

"But … they will have to wait until after our road trip," he announced.

C.J. smiled. "Cool."

"Road trip?" asked Raine. "What road trip?"

"Every school break," C.J. explained, "one of us gets to ride with Dad on his route."

Raine knew that Uncle Greg was a truck driver working for a company out of Grand Rapids, but she didn't realize that Uncle Greg took her cousins with him sometimes. "Most of the time, I haul locally," Uncle Greg explained. "But occasionally the company receives long haul jobs. I volunteer to take the big loads during school breaks to earn extra money."

"This Christmas break, it's finally my turn," chimed in C.J.

"Speaking of which … " Uncle Greg directed his attention toward Raine and Cille. "… how do you two feel about coming along for the ride this time?"

"Us?" Raine gave it some thought and scowled. "Why? But what about my parents?"

They were interrupted when a large basket of fries arrived at the table. The waitress brought small plates for them. C.J. was the first to load his plate and douse ketchup all over his food. The waitress smiled. "Anything else?"

"No, thanks. Just the bill." Uncle Greg popped a hot French fry in his mouth and then whispered, "Look, there is something I need to tell you kids. As you know, Uncle Larry, Uncle Ronald, and Aunt Agnes disappeared in November. Their plane was last seen over the Bermuda Triangle. Your grandpa and cousins were on their way to Washington D.C. to get some answers when their plane also disappeared."

"Why did our cousins go?" asked Cille.

Raine sat with her arms crossed. "I heard that they took off in the middle of night in search of their parents." *Oddly enough, Aunt Adelaide's cat hasn't been seen since then either which made her great-aunt's story believable.*

C.J. pushed up his glasses. "I heard aliens landed on Uncle Ronald's farm and abducted them."

"Nonsense. They have not been abducted by aliens." Uncle Greg wrapped two hands around his glass. "We are confident that they will be found. Meanwhile, Raine, your dad had to go to Washington D.C. to help with the investigation. Your mom said its okay for you to go with me while she takes care of Aunt Adelaide."

Raine had just seen her dad this morning. "He couldn't wait to say goodbye? And it's Christmas break!"

"It was a sudden request," Uncle Greg said. "He was offered a private jet to the East Coast."

That didn't make Raine feel better. She bit her lip.

Uncle Greg continued. "You can take a truck ride." He paused. "Unless, you would like to stay with your mom and help her out with your great aunt."

Raine did a quick rundown of her choices. She really liked spending time with her mom and great-aunt, but she didn't want to be cooped up at home all break long. A road trip sounded better. She looked at Cille. "What about Cille?" Raine said.

"Yeah, what about me?" Cille said. "Can I come, too?"

"I already cleared it with your parents," Uncle Greg said. "You haven't had an attack in a long time and they've explained what I should do if that happens."

"I know I'll be fine," Cille said. "Yes!" She hardly ever got to go anywhere with other people because her parents worried she might have an epileptic seizure. But they could certainly trust Uncle Greg to take care of her.

"It's settled," Greg said. "Since we're in town, we will swing by your house first, Raine. You can pack. Then we will get Cille's stuff. You'll stay at my place tonight so we can get an early start."

"All right!" C.J. said. "Slumber party!"

"No, you will go to bed. We have to be up at 5 a.m."

A spray of cherry coke came out of Raine's mouth "Five in the morning! Tomorrow?"

"Yeah," said Uncle Greg casually. "We've got a long way to go."

Raine was starting to regret her decision. "Where are we going again, and how long are we going to be gone exactly? Will we be back for

Christmas?"

Uncle Greg reassured her that everyone would be back in time. "Des Moines, Iowa." He dropped some cash on the table to pay the bill. "Two nights tops." He started to zip his coat and put on his driving gloves.

"Iowa? Doesn't it snow there?" asked Raine as they all stood from the table. She put on her coat too.

"No more than it snows in Michigan," Uncle Greg explained as they headed out of the restaurant. "If the weather stays good, we will drive straight to Des Moines. We'll drop my load, spend the night, and pick up another. We should be home in a couple days."

Uncle Greg drove everyone to Raine's house so she could get her things. Her mom greeted them at the door and then pulled her daughter upstairs. She gave the young girl a stern private talk about being suspended from school and reminded Raine that this road trip was not a reward. Her punishment would come when she returned. Being that said Alexandria gave her daughter a big hug and told her how much she would miss her. She then gave some packing instructions as she was leaving the bedroom.

Cille entered shortly. "Is the coast clear?"

Raine gestured her cousin in. "I love your

room," said Cille as she walked into the cluttered catastrophe.

Raine smiled. Cille said that every time. Raine and her mom had recently painted her bedroom with her favorite colors—lime green and purple.

Cille lived in a much smaller house. "I just feel like I am in another time or place in this house," Cille said. "It's like an old mansion, except for your room, of course."

Raine knew that Cille had a fantastic imagination. Her cousin loved to write and act. She dreamed of being a famous writer or actress someday. Raine, on the other hand, didn't have a particular dream.

Well, maybe she dreamed of staying at one place for longer than a couple years. She wished her dad had a normal stay-at-home job. Her mom, now being caretaker of the Helldemueller House, was the closest thing to having a stay-at-home mom. Raine sighed and reminded herself to not get attached to this house. They were only renting it, after all.

Raine grabbed her oversized purple duffle bag and started throwing in clothes. What should she pack for a two-day road trip anyway?

As Raine was zipping up her bag, Aunt Adelaide walked in. "Here, this would be good reading material for you." She handed her the large family book.

"I thought this book was supposed to be kept here in the house and safe."

"As long as you wear that necklace, I think all will be protected. And it might be best to keep it hidden from your uncle. He's not very fond of the book." Aunt Adelaide hugged Raine. "I will miss you."

"You too," mumbled Raine.

Aunt Adelaide reached out unsteadily for Cille "And you too."

"Geez, you girls act like we are leaving for good or something," declared C.J. as he walked in. "We will be back in two days. Come on, dad is asking if you are ready yet."

As she walked downstairs with her bags packed, Raine wondered what would be in store for her next.

The CB report

Soon after they arrived at Uncle Greg's house, their aunt Tricia came over. She was staying at C.J.'s house to watch the three younger brothers. Their aunt had no kids of her own and helped out a lot since C.J.'s mom died.

Uncle Greg put some frozen pizzas in the oven for dinner. While the food was baking, C.J. gave Raine a quick tour of his home. It was the first time that Raine had been there. His house was smaller than the Helldemueller House. It was a ranch-style with the basics: a kitchen, dining area, living room, three bedrooms, and two bathrooms. It also had a finished basement. The kids sprawled out in the basement family room while they ate their dinner. They decided to watch a movie on an old projection TV.

"I think I'm getting nervous about

tomorrow?" said Cille as she grabbed her pizza and reached for her journal. She was excited to have something cool like the road trip to journal about, but her stomach was filling with butterflies.

"Why?" asked Raine as she lay in a sleeping bag.

"You'll be fine, Cille," C.J. said through a mouthful of food. "You haven't had a seizure in a year."

"I know," Cille replied. "It isn't that, really. Maybe I'm worried about getting car sick. It's a long time on the road." Cille burrowed herself into her sleeping bag. The basement was cold. "I haven't been away from home in a long time."

Raine couldn't relate, but she knew what to say. "Hey, C.J. is right. You'll be with us—the Three Deams! It will be like a mini-vacation. While other kids are stuck in school for a couple more days, we get to see the country and eat junk food in a big semi." Raine reached into her backpack, "And I have this!" She pulled out *The Prophecies and Powers of Trahe.*

Cille perked up. "Does Aunt Adelaide know?"

"It was her idea to take it," Raine replied, "so long as I promised to take really good care of it. And get this, she said, 'Keep it hidden from Uncle Greg.'"

"Why do you think she wants us to hide it from my dad?" C.J. said.

"I don't know," Raine shrugged. "She didn't say."

Greg walked into the basement. "Kids, all settled in for the night?"

Raine startled. She hadn't heard him come down the stairs. She quickly shoved the book back in her bag.

"Gee, Dad," complained C.J. "Don't sneak up on us like that. You scared us."

"I didn't sneak. Are you watching a scary movie or something?" Before they could answer, Greg continued, "Don't be up too late. Remember, we leave at 5 a.m. sharp!" He headed back upstairs and flicked the light on and off while making ghostly sounds. "Good night!"

The girls laughed, but C.J. just rolled his eyes.

Five a.m. came too early. The kids grumbled and rolled in their sleeping bags as Greg tried to wake them up. "If you'd rather stay here and work on the Evadeam farm instead, that's fine with me." That got them moving, and they were ready to leave in less than thirty minutes.

"This truck is huge," said Cille as she climbed into the big rig. Uncle Greg typically drove a smaller semi-truck for his weekly short hauls. But for this trip, his company had given him one with a larger sleeper cab. "Where do I sit?"

It was still dark outside, but the cab of the truck was brightly lit. It had two huge seats, a big dashboard with compartments above the windshield and by the floor. Behind the front seats were tiny closets on each side. One stored a TV. Then there was a long back seat that folded down to a bed. Above that was another bunk that folded down with overhead storage bins.

"I thought you kids could take turns riding in front," Greg explained.

"Since this is really your trip, C.J.," said Cille, "why don't you take the first turn?"

Raine agreed, and the girls went toward the back of the cab. Uncle Greg and C.J. handed them the bags. The girls put them away while Uncle Greg mumbled something about the kids packing too much. He would be surprised if it all fit. It did ... barely.

After much shoving, grunting, and repacking, they were off. First they were headed to Uncle Greg's workplace in Grand Rapids to pick up their load. They picked up an aluminum trailer of packaged goods. Before they hit the highway, C.J. complained he was hungry.

"Already?" his father said.

"I didn't eat breakfast. You rushed us this morning, so I didn't have time."

Greg sighed and glanced into his rearview mirror. "I suppose you girls are hungry, too?"

Raine didn't answer, but Cille put her hand to her stomach. "Maybe."

"Okay, but we have to get out of the city first. I need to pull into a restaurant where I can park a semi."

Cille felt the grinding of the gears as the truck pulled onto U.S. Highway 131, heading south. The eighteen-wheeler was loud, but aside from the noise, the cab was comfortable. Cille peered out a small rear window, which had a curtain that could be pulled for privacy. She glanced over to her cousin to see that she was also enjoying the scenery.

Raine loved riding high in the truck. She watched as cars whizzed by them and was surprised by how many vehicles passed and cut them off. *Don't they know this truck can't stop suddenly and would crush them?* Luckily, Uncle Greg was an excellent driver.

Uncle Greg wanted to reach Walcott, Iowa by 3 p.m. so he would be on track to drop off his load in Des Moines no later than the next morning. Then he needed to pick up another load there that needed to be delivered back in Michigan.

They grabbed some fast food breakfast just outside of Grand Rapids and by the time they hit Kalamazoo, Cille was ready for a bathroom break.

They merged onto I-94 West and watched for the first rest area sign. "Make it quick," Uncle Greg said as he pulled into a rest stop. All the kids went to the bathrooms and returned to the cab hastily. As Cille pulled herself up, she noticed a golden retriever puppy running back and forth across the grass. It was barking, and Cille didn't see anyone with the dog. "Do you think the puppy is lost?"

Uncle Greg was looking at a weather report on his phone. Without glancing toward the dog, he said, "I am sure it's with one of the visitors here. People are always traveling with their pets. They let them out here for potty breaks." He broke away from his phone and turned to them. "All set?"

Cille nodded, even though she bit her bottom lip, she was still worried about the puppy. As she buckled her seat belt, Raine leaned toward her. "I'm sure Uncle Greg's right. The puppy's owner is here somewhere."

"But what if it's lost like Cleo?" As they drove away, Cille had a nagging feeling that she was right. She watched the puppy as it barked and ran from person to person with no one seeming to claim it.

Raine watched, too, and saw the puppy chase the semi. Then, the puppy was out of sight. She closed her eyes and did a silent prayer for it. When she opened her eyes, she noticed white snowflakes coming down outside. The few flakes soon developed into flurries. As they drove closer toward Lake Michigan, the snowfall became heavier.

Cille tightened her seat belt. She was getting another bad feeling.

"Is something wrong?" Raine asked, noticing that Cille seemed uneasy.

"No," Cille said, "everything's fine." Though she couldn't explain why she was getting nervous. It didn't seem to be about the snow.

"Come on," Uncle Greg urged to a vehicle in front of them. "A little snow makes people forget how to drive in Michigan."

Raine felt the truck slow down and heard a sound from inside the cab. It was the CB radio.

Uncle Greg reached over and turned up the volume.

"Truckers still have CB radios?" asked Raine.

"Yeah," whispered C.J., "but Dad uses his cell phone, blue tooth and GPS mostly. The CB is used for accident, weather, and bear reports," C.J. explained. "I even have my own handle—Batman."

The radio crackled. *Hi, Westbound I-94 truckers. Accident. Four-wheelers at yardstick 32.*

Uncle Greg grabbed the mic. "Breaker, breaker. One nine for a radio check. Joker, over."

This is Uncle Sam, someone said in reply. *Your*

radio is clear. Over.

"Thank you. How backed up is I-94 Westbound?"

Just starting to pile up at yardstick 32. Full-grown bears and wannabes on the scene.

Cille lowered her voice so Uncle Greg could listen to the report. "Bears?!"

C.J. turned in his seat. "Cops. Full-grown bears are state police or Department of Transportation officers. Wannabes are other police officers."

Uncle Greg placed the mic back on the radio. "We might be stuck in this truck for a while."

When they got closer to the scene, the traffic wasn't too backed up yet, so they stayed on the freeway. Eventually they could see the police cars and the accident. Cille looked away when she saw the back-end of a crushed vehicle and stared straight ahead through the large cab window.

They had just passed the accident scene when suddenly a small red car zipped by in the left lane. It cut off a van in the right lane. The van slammed its breaks, spun out into a ditch, flipping onto its side. Uncle Greg braked the truck. The kids shifted against their seatbelts from the sudden change in speed. Raine watched the front of their truck come dangerously close to the ditch.

"Sorry about that," Uncle Greg said hastily.

He grabbed the CB mic and reported the new accident while the red car raced away. He put on his flashers. "Kids, stay in the truck. It's too dangerous out there. I've got to help." He let himself out of the cab.

As Cille watched Uncle Greg run toward the overturned van, she suddenly became overcome with a sinking feeling. She stared at her lap. She didn't want to watch. The image of the van disturbed her.

Raine noticed Cille turning pale. "It's okay, Cille. I'm sure everyone is fine. Uncle Greg is helping."

Cille said nothing.

C.J. glanced back at Cille. "Uh-oh. She's doing it again."

"Doing what?" Raine asked. "Is she having a seizure? Oh no!"

"No, it's not that," Cille said quickly. She felt light-headed. A deep feeling told her that someone had died in the van.

"What are you seeing?" C.J. asked.

Raine interrupted, "How could she see anything? She is not even looking outside?"

"That's not what I meant," replied C.J. "Something is wrong out there."

Raine was confused, but Cille reassured her that she was okay. Cille looked outside when she heard the sirens of emergency vehicles arriving at the scene. Their flashing lights reflected against the windows. A chill went through her. She slowly turned toward Raine's side of the truck. Then it dawned on her. She wasn't cold because of the temperature in the cab. Through the window, she could see a reflection of a man dressed in a worn coat and wearing a knitted cap—but Cille knew this man was dead.

"Cille, are you sure you are okay? Car sickness? An attack coming on?" asked Raine. "Your face is really pale?"

C.J. turned to look at her. "Cille?"

The man pointed in the direction of the ditch.

"Ghost," Cille whispered.

Talking Dead

Raine peered through the window. "Ghost?! What are you talking about? Cille, you're not making any sense." Raine peered through the window and tried to see what was making Cille's face turn the same color as a puked up marshmallow.

C.J. locked the truck doors. "How many are there?"

"Just one," Cille said, keeping her gaze down.

"What? One what?" Raine looked back and forth between her cousins and the window.

At that moment, someone knocked on the driver's side window. The kids screamed. Uncle Greg knocked some more. His voice was muffled from the glass. "Unlock the door."

C.J. followed orders. His dad jumped into the driver's seat.

C.J. pointed to Cille. "Dad."

"Honey, you all right?" He had noticed Cille's ashen face.

"She saw one. You know—a ghost," C.J. said. "Did someone die in the crash?"

"Uh-huh," Cille replied.

Raine noticed that her uncle did not seem phased by the word *ghost*. Uncle Greg opened up the cooler between the two seats. He pulled out a water bottle and handed it to Cille. "Drink. It'll be okay."

As Cille drank the cool liquid with shaky hands, Uncle Greg whispered, "What exactly did you see?"

No one spoke for a moment. Cille took a deep breath and then pointed toward the truck window. "There was a man looking at me. He's not there anymore." She looked at Raine. "I see ghosts. Spirits. It's my Evadeam curse."

"It's not a curse," Uncle Greg said softly. "It's a gift." He put a reassuring hand on Cille's knee.

"Um, people — you are talking about seeing ghosts!" cried Raine.

"Yeah, and you thought I was crazy claiming aliens landed on our uncle's farm," said C.J.

Raine looked back and forth between her cousins and uncle. Their faces told her that they really believed. She shifted towards Cille. "Ghosts? You think you see ghosts and you never bothered to say anything before now?" Raine asked, with a hint of anger in her voice.

"It isn't something I like to brag about. Besides, would you have believed me?" Cille paused, "as you said "you think I see ghosts"".

Raine thought about the book and the family rumors. Ghosts, messengers, spirits, gifts, curses, and aliens. She always thought it was nonsense until her great-aunt handed her the family book. Now her two favorite cousins—her BFFs—were saying Cille could see ghosts. Even Uncle Greg was, too. She did not know what to believe. She could think it was just a joke, but Uncle Greg's composure told her it wasn't.

"Raine, there's a lot that your dad should be telling you. About our family. It's not my place, but considering the circumstances, let's just say that we have some family members who have special gifts. Cille is one of them. It doesn't make her different or odd—just special." He smiled at Cille and then looked at Raine. "She is still the same Cille, you know. Still your friend."

Raine didn't know what to say.

C.J. spoke up. "Yeah, it's okay. There's something cool about seeing ghosts. And you don't have to be afraid. None of them have been scary. They usually just want to deliver a message. Right, Cille?"

Cille nodded.

"Does this one have a message?" asked Uncle Greg.

"He pointed toward the ditch." Cille's eyes widened as she looked out of Raine's frosty window. "He's back. Quick, Uncle Greg! The ditch. He said his son was thrown from the van. He is lying near a drain where no one can see him."

Uncle Greg didn't hesitate to hop out of the truck.

The kids stayed quiet in the truck. All Raine could hear was their breathing. The windows were frosting over. Raine noticed a handprint on the window. She scooted next to Cille. Maybe there was a ghost.

"That's him," whispered Cille.

"What does he want?" Raine was starting to believe the ghost story as she looked at the mark on the glass.

"He is sad. He had been driving the van. They just stopped for fuel. He forgot to put his seat belt back on. He's worried — he's not ready to cross over."

"So what do we do?" asked Raine as she sat even closer to Cille. "Can he hurt us?"

C.J. answered, "No. He won't hurt us. Grandpa always said that the best way to handle a lost ghost is to pray." He held out his hands. "Come on."

The three kids grabbed each other's hands as C.J. prayed. "Dear God, please shine your light around us and Dad. Please protect us. Please watch over us and enfold your love around us. And *please* protect this lost spirit. Please guide Dad to find the man's son and help the spirit find you. Thank you, Lord. Amen."

They sat there in silence until Uncle Greg came back. Raine noticed that Uncle Greg was red-faced from the cold air. He climbed into his seat. "I found a boy in the ditch. He's alive but he hadn't been wearing his seatbelt. He's the man's son. Paramedics say he'll be okay. "

Raine stared at the handprint again and watched it fade away. Now she believed Cille, just like everyone else. The CB radio crackled, and they heard a man's voice whisper, "Thank you."

Everyone froze.

"Ghosts sometimes can communicate through electronics," whispered Cille. "It's him."

"You're welcome," Uncle Greg replied loudly.

The noise from the CB stopped.

"He's gone," announced Cille. She sat back in her seat and wondered if the incident would change her friendship with Raine. She wasn't sure if Raine was a believer. And if she was now, Cille was pretty sure that Raine was freaked out. Cille didn't blame her. Who wants to be friends with an epileptic clairvoyant? Cille gulped down some more water.

Time ticked by until a knock on the truck made all of them jump. Uncle Greg rolled down the window. A state trooper thanked Greg for his help. "I'm curious, how did you know about the kid?"

"Let's just call it a gut feeling," Greg said.

The state trooper nodded and peered into the cab.

Raine could see the trooper's face from her seat. She recognized him as a local who attended their church.

The trooper noticed the children and said hello. "Hey Raine," he said offhand, "I heard from my son that you stood up to that boy Gideon and got in big trouble for it. You know, we are having an anti-bullying meeting for our teen group at church in January. Sure would like it if you attended."

"Okay." She didn't really want to go, but what else was she going to say to a uniformed officer?

"Good." He put a gloved hand through the window and shook Uncle Greg's hand. "Thanks again. Wish we had more folks willing to help out like your family. We will be opening up the highway again as soon as the ambulances clear."

The officer walked away and shortly thereafter emergency units started to pull away.

Before they continued on, Uncle Greg leaned back in his seat and sighed. "Kids, you want to go on or go back home? I will totally understand if you want to call it quits."

"You're still going with this snowstorm?" asked Raine.

"Yep, but I should turn around and get you kids back safely."

Cille spoke up. "No." Her shoulders sagged. "The ghost had a message before he left. He said that we need to continue. It's important that we move forward."

C.J. watched his dad's facial expressions. "I think we should keep going, too. Besides, the weather report on the CB says the storm is moving towards Nashville."

"Raine?" asked Uncle Greg.

She hated being put on the spot. She wished she were home in her cozy bed. Their adventure hadn't been fun. It had actually been quite scary. But either way she looked at it, she didn't want to ruin everything for everyone else, and Raine was anything but a coward. "I'm in."

"Sure?" asked her uncle.

"Yeah," she said firmly.

Her uncle hesitated.

"Really, it's okay," assured Raine.

A few minutes later, the eighteen-wheeler

rolled back onto the freeway. No one spoke in the cab. Each was deep in their own thoughts.

As Raine watched the snow swirl around outside, she remembered arguments her parents had about her dad's family. Raine had perfected the art of eavesdropping. At the time, the conversations hadn't made sense to her. Now they did. Her dad was always wanting to tell Raine about the family ... the secrets. Her mom would say no. No wonder. The Evadeam clan was a strange breed.

Raine brought her thoughts back to the present. Maybe she had to accept the fact that she was part of an eccentric family with too many *real* secrets. "So Uncle Greg, do we have any ghost hunters in our family?"

He laughed but didn't answer. C.J., however, jumped on the opportunity to talk about the subject. "As a matter of fact, I heard that we have a second cousin ..."

And that was the beginning of the Evadeam family history crash course taught by C.J. Evadeam. Raine was not sure what to believe, but she enjoyed the tales of alien abductions, talking ghosts, and other stories. As the truck moved on, Raine noticed that Cille had fallen asleep. Raine started to feel tired, too, but curiosity kept her awake as she listened to C.J. Soon her eyelids got heavy. She nodded off for a moment until her cell phone woke her. It was her dad. She hadn't spoken to her parents since they had left. The phone stopped ringing before she got a chance to answer it. She decided to text him.

Sorry. Missed call.

He immediately text back. *You okay?*

Yeah. She hesitated and decided to go for it. *We had an incident. We're ok. But what can you tell me about the Evadeam gift? As in seeing dead people?*

He didn't answer. Uncle Greg's phone rang. Raine watched as Uncle Greg answered with his blue tooth headset. He glanced back at Raine, and then cautiously filled his brother in.

Raine's fingers started typing again. *Dad, don't yell at Uncle Greg. I'm ok. I guess it's time for me to know the truth. Tell me the truth.*

A few minutes later, Uncle Greg hung up his phone, and Raine got a call from her dad.

"We will talk more when I get home," her father said. "I don't want to get into it over the phone."

"Dad. Just tell me, is it true? Does Cille have a special gift?"

Her father paused. "Yeah, Raine. I'm sorry, but I am at work and have to go. You are safe with Uncle Greg. I love you, Raine. See you soon."

"Love you, too, Dad." Raine stared at her phone as she let the words "you are safe with Uncle

Greg" sink in. What did that mean?

Raine's stomach churned. She felt tears developing in her eyes. She really could use a break.

As if reading her mind, Uncle Greg announced that they were getting off at the next exit to stop for gas and re-group. As they pulled off the highway, the sun peeked out from behind a cloud. Raine felt a moment of calmness.

I-80 Truck Stop

Two hours later, Cille opened her eyes to find herself slumped against the cab window. The emotional toll from the earlier incident and the ride had left her weary. As she yawned and stretched, she noticed that her cousins were playing on their portable gaming systems. Cille smoothed her hair with her hands and drank from a bottle of water to wake herself up.

Uncle Greg noticed Cille had awoken. "Welcome back, sleepyhead. How do you feel?"

"Okay. Where are we?"

"Illinois, near Joliet." They had a long haul ahead and he wanted to get through Chicago traffic before rush hour.

Cille peered out the window and saw an Interstate 80 sign. She was always fond of maps and grabbed the atlas to find their location. They must have crossed Indiana and switched highways while she was sleeping. They were close to Chicago. She watched as her uncle punched in an address into his GPS system.

"I'm hungry," mumbled C.J. as he stretched taking off his ear phones.

"You're always hungry," piped up Raine turning off her own electronics.

"What about you, girls?" asked Uncle Greg.

Cille glanced at all the junk food wrappers from what they had eaten earlier. She wasn't hungry at all. "Not really."

"Me either," said Raine.

"Well, I am," said C.J. again.

"Tell you what. I've got some apples in the refrigerator. Eat an apple to tie you over, C.J. I want to keep going. There's another storm coming. I want to get to Walcott before it starts. We can have a big dinner at the Iowa 80 truck stop."

"Cool!" agreed C.J.

"What is so cool about a truck stop?" Cille asked.

"It's the largest one I've ever seen," C.J. said. "It's my favorite!"

"How cool can a truck stop be?" mumbled Raine.

"You'll see," C.J. said.

As predicted, snow started to come down

hard. Uncle Greg groaned again. "Maybe I should have left you kids at home."

"It's okay, Uncle Greg," Cille said. "This is an adventure, remember?"

The kids decided to start a *Harry Potter* movie marathon to pass the time, and a few hours later, Uncle Greg pulled off at an exit and parked at the Iowa 80 truck stop. "We made it."

"It's about time," said C.J. "I think I could eat a whole cow."

Raine took in the scene outside. The travel center was huge.

"You will have plenty of food to choose from," Uncle Greg said. "There is a restaurant with a salad bar. But if you don't want that, there's always the food court."

"Let's hit the salad bar," suggested Cille.

"Good choice," Uncle Greg said. They bundled up and walked toward the building. Uncle Greg opened the doors for the girls. "There's also a store, private showers, a movie theater, a game room—they even have their own museum."

Raine smiled as she walked in. This was no ordinary truck center as she eyed everything her uncle had mentioned. They quickly used the bathrooms and went to the restaurant.

Raine smelled burgers on the grill. She didn't realize how hungry she had gotten. Skip the salad bar—she sure could go for a cheeseburger. She wondered if they had green olives and bacon to add. Soon, they were sitting down and ordering dinner. Cille ordered from the salad bar.

"Make sure to get the fat-free salad dressing, Cille," smirked C.J. "For me, I am ordering a hot, juicy burger from the Midwest. With fries and a chocolate shake."

"I've already eaten too much junk food," Cille complained.

Uncle Greg ordered steak, potatoes, and salad from the waitress.

The waitress asked where they were headed.

"Des Moines," offered Uncle Greg.

"Good. Not too far," she said. "We have a snowstorm coming, you know."

"What's the forecast saying now?"

"Could get as much as twelve inches," the waitress said.

"Twelve inches?" Uncle Greg said in surprise. "When we were near Chicago, they were only expecting three. What's going on?"

The waitress shrugged. "Don't look at me." She pointed a thumb toward the window. "It's starting to come down now."

The waitress was right. Raine saw snow coming down like rain. She could barely see the parking lot. She glanced at Uncle Greg, who pulled out his phone to check on the weather again. "We might be here for a while. The waitress is right."

When they were done eating dinner, C.J. asked if they could order dessert, too.

"Are you kidding me?" said Cille. "I'm stuffed. How could you want more food?"

"Don't you know I'm a growing boy?"

"Kids, order what you want," said Uncle Greg. "We've got time."

"All right!" C.J. looked at the menu. "Cake, brownie sundae, or homemade pie."

"I doubt it is homemade," stated Raine.

"How about the Dairy Queen in the food court?" suggested Cille.

"Great," said C.J.. "We can eat dessert here, go to a movie, play games, and then visit the Dairy Queen."

Cille giggled.

Just then, Raine noticed police officers pass by their table. She watched as the cops stopped at a booth on the other side of the room. Raine hadn't paid attention to the family that had been sitting there until now. There was a man, a woman, and two young girls. She noticed that the children looked embarrassed and shifted uncomfortably. The woman seemed upset, and the man was starting to get mad. He raised his voice. "What are we supposed to do? It's cold out there."

Raine's attention to the family was interrupted by their waitress. "Dessert?"

As they placed their orders, Uncle Greg also noticed the conversation between the family and police. As the waitress went to take his order, he whispered to her. "Any idea what's going on over there?"

The waitress leaned down. "It's sad. The dad was laid off from his job in Michigan. They lost everything. You know—their home. They packed up all they had left and came all the way here for a job in Des Moines. They moved into a hotel until he could earn enough money for an apartment. But that auto business shut down too, and now they're stranded here with no money."

"Homeless?" Cille asked.

"Yes, sweetie. They've been living here in the truck stop. Ordering and splitting meals, using our showers, and sleeping in their van. They have nowhere to go. They tried the homeless shelters, but they're full."

"So why the cops?" asked Uncle Greg.

"Because they didn't order anything. Just water, so the manager wants them to leave. They're hogging up a table." She lowered her voice even more. "He called the local sheriff to have them kicked off the premises."

"But it's snowing," said Cille.

"I know, but what can you do?" She straightened. "I better get your order in."

Raine help up a hand. "Wait. Give my dessert to the family instead."

"Ah, that is sweet of you," said the waitress. "But the manager isn't going to like that. They can only stay if they're paying customers."

"Tell you what," Uncle Greg said. "You kids get your dessert." He handed a fifty-dollar bill to the waitress. "Use this to get that family a meal. This is their money now. They're customers."

"Wow," said the waitress. "That is kind of you. I will tell them right now."

When she did, the two officers and the family looked their way. The dad started to get up to return the money, but Uncle Greg waved him down and lifted up his cup in salute. With that, the family got to stay and eat.

Their dessert came, and Cille stared at her cheesecake. "You know, we don't need to go to the movie theater. We have movies in the truck." She felt bad spending more of Uncle Greg's money.

"Yeah," said C.J. as he bit into his brownie. "And I don't have to play games."

"Hey, Uncle Greg!" Raine said. "Didn't my mom give you money for an adjoining hotel room for Cille and me? Maybe you can give that money to the family, and we can all share one room."

Uncle Greg nodded with a smile. "We could do that."

"I don't mind sharing a room with you and C.J.," Raine continued. "If we get a room with two beds, then Cille and I can share a bed."

"Yep," Cille agreed.

"Where am I going to sleep?" asked C.J. "I'm way too old to sleep with Dad."

"I bet we can order a rollaway bed," Raine said before taking a sip of her strawberry shake.

"I'll check with your parents. I'm sure it's okay," said Uncle Greg. "Sure you girls don't mind?"

They didn't, and so they agreed to give the extra hotel money to the family. Uncle Greg went over to their booth, introduced himself, and offered them the money for the hotel. The parents tried to object, but their girls interrupted. They hugged their father. "Please, Daddy," one said tearfully. "Let's go. I don't want to stay here anymore."

Uncle Greg reassured them that a future payback would be for them to return kindness to someone else someday.

The father slowly agreed. Before leaving the table, Uncle Greg exchanged names and information with him. Greg said he would check to see if his company was hiring. The man thanked him.

Raine watched as the family ate and savored

every bite. She felt good and guilty at the same time. She knew the economy was bad. Her own mother had been laid off before moving to Nashville. And Raine had a place called home. She still had stuff and clothes. She could even afford to buy a candy bar. She then had an idea and wondered what she had in the truck that she could give the two girls. She shared her idea with Cille who agreed.

"I over packed anyway," Cille said.

Uncle Greg checked his phone again. "Well, that's odd. The weather people can't seem to make up their minds. Now they're only forecasting six inches." He glanced at the windows. "And sure enough, it's hardly snowing out there again." He smiled. "Good news, kids. We can still make it to Des Moines tonight."

"But what about the movie theater?" C.J. asked.

"We'll just continue our *Harry Potter* marathon in the truck," Raine suggested.

As they got up to go, the waitress came back with their bill.

"Thanks," said Uncle Greg as he paid and gave the waitress a big tip.

"Thank you. You're good people. What you did for that family was mighty fine. God will take care of you. In fact, I think he's looking over that family." She rested her hands on her hips. "What are the chances of you being here at the exact same time that they're about to be kicked out to the curb? It was meant to be." She took the money and walked away humming.

Cille thought about what the waitress had said. Today was no coincidence. "Hey, remember what the ghost said? We were supposed to come here."

"Whoa! That is right," said C.J. "See? It was meant to be."

Raine absorbed the information. Maybe the waitress and Cille were right.

"Everyone ready?" asked Uncle Greg.

"Yeah," said Raine, "but can Cille and I go through our bags and give something to the girls?"

"Hey," C.J. said, "Maybe there's something I brought, too, that they can have. Like my books or something."

"Yeah," Cille said. "That's a great idea. It's almost Christmas. How are they going to have a great Christmas?"

"Kids, how about we get them something new from the gift shop?" Uncle Greg suggested. "Everyone can pick something out."

The girls still insisted on donating one of their own clothes. Then, they bought some items from the store. Even the restaurant manager broke down and donated I-80 truck stop souvenir t-shirts for each family member. The manager turned to Uncle Greg and handed him a bag. "Thanks for your generosity and a friendly lesson for myself on kindness." He also gave blue souvenir t-shirts to Uncle Greg and C.J.—pink shirts for the girls.

"Cool!" exclaimed C.J.

Uncle Greg shook the manager's hand. "Thank you, every little bit helps. Maybe they can get assistance in Des Moines." After visiting the gift shop, Greg walked over to the table to see if the family wanted to follow them to Des Moines. Uncle Greg offered to pay for their gas. *Maybe once they were in Des Moines, they could call the local services there or a church for help.*

The dad hesitated and looked embarrassed when Uncle Greg gave them the bags of items they had purchased. But Uncle Greg insisted. "Generosity comes full circle," he said. "It's my family's turn to give. Now let's get some gas." The mother reached for the bags and thanked him profusely. She whispered to her husband, "This family's kindness is nothing short of a miracle, and that's what we need right now."

The father looked at his family, and suddenly gave Uncle Greg a big hug

And the Three Deams couldn't have been more pleased.

Moments later, Raine looked out the truck

window as they left the parking lot. "How long is the drive, Uncle Greg?"

"Depends if Old Man Winter is holding his breath or if he is going to blow in some more snow. GPS says two and a half hours."

Raine thought about her first visit to the infamous Iowa 80 truck stop, and the family that followed behind them to Des Moines. She hadn't gotten a chance to check out the theater, the video arcade, or the museum; but what she had experienced was much better than that. What they were doing for the family was just like the mother had said, a miracle—the second miracle they helped create today when she thought of the rescued boy.

She smiled and leaned back in her seat. "Hey, you guys ready to finish watching *Harry Potter 2*?"

Sixth Sense

The sun was setting early in Des Moines, so they arrived after nightfall. While the kids waited in the truck, Uncle Greg helped check the stranded family into the hotel. The father shook Uncle Greg's hand and thanked him again. After they were taken care of, Uncle Greg hurried to get his truck load to the business before it closed. Then, they picked up the new load so they would be ready to head back to Michigan first thing in the morning.

Uncle Greg and the kids returned to the hotel and checked into a suite that was available. Raine walked into the room with appreciation. First, they entered into a living area with a sleeper sofa. Raine and Cille agreed to sleep there. C.J. and his dad took the two double beds in the adjacent room.

Once they were settled in for the night, Cille called her parents to say goodnight. Raine also decided to check in with her mom. Raine told her all about their road trip escapades. Raine decided to leave out the supernatural stuff. By now, she knew mom was not a fan of the Evadeam family secrets and talents. After talking with her mom, she asked to speak with Aunt Adelaide. Raine talked quickly filling her aunt in with all the ghostly details. "Did you know about Cille's gift?"

"Yes dear, but it was not my secret to tell. Almost all of the Evadeams have a special gift or talent. Some not so extreme." Aunt Adelaide paused for a moment "Raine, your gift could be simply being caretaker of the family book. Or perhaps having the sixth sense. And as for Cille, she is your cousin and friend. She will need your friendship and strength."

"Okay Aunt Adelaide."

"Now, you have a good night and see you soon dear."

A picture of a black and white cat formed into Raine's head. "Wait, has Cleo come home yet?"

"No, that little rascal is still missing. But don't you worry. I am sure that she is safe with my brother and your cousins."

Raine had momentarily forgotten all about her missing family members. Life was busy and had continued for her. Her eyes wandered to her back pack. She wanted to read the book before they went to bed. She said her goodbyes, but before reaching for the book she decided to text her dad again. She knew he was busy, so she thought best not to call him.

She texted him about the family from the truck stop.

He replied quickly. *You have officially experienced an Evadeam spiritual miracle—or Christmas miracle. Not so bad, is it?*

Not so bad. Raine smiled. She was happy to be talking to her dad again even if it was through texting. She changed the subject to other things. *Will you be back for Christmas?*

Definitely!

Good because if you are not, then, I am returning your Christmas gift.

Her dad sent back a smiley face. *I gotta go. Love you, Raine. Have a good night.*

Love you, too, Dad. Night.

Raine was walking toward her bags when Uncle Greg peered into their adjacent room. "Kids, don't stay up too late," Uncle Greg said. "C.J., I'm going to call your brothers before bed. You wanna talk to them?"

"Nah," replied C.J.

"Suit yourself," his father said.

After everyone got ready for bed, the girls and C.J. sat on the sofa bed.

"Raine, can I see the book?" asked Cille.

"Sure."

Raine pulled it out of her bag, and Cille turned the pages quickly as if searching for something. She stopped and a concerned look appeared on her face.

"What is it?" asked Raine.

Cille held up the book. On the page was a drawing of a puppy. On the other side of the page was the picture of the ghost she saw.

"Whoa!" exclaimed C.J.

Raine pulled out her necklace that was tucked under her shirt. She grasped it with her right hand while her other hand turned the page. A picture of what looked like the I-80 truck stop was revealed. Raine quickly let go. She was starting to freak out inside. *She should be use to these surprises by now.*

C.J. leaned over the book "I don't get it. I thought this book was about other family members like our missing cousins. But now it seems to be writing about our adventures."

Cille turned the page and it was blank. She flipped the pages backwards and stopped. "I don't remember seeing this before." She then smiled after reading a particular page. "Look."

She held the open book toward C.J. and Raine.

On the left page, C.J. saw a printed drawing

of an angel illuminated by light. On the right side of the book was printed text.

Raine read it aloud.

The Creator breathed life into different forms of beings and gave special powers to those marked as messengers, prophets, and seers. These spiritual guides were positioned all over the world. Over time, these gifted beings gave birth to children who were born with powers. Some of the human form children had heightened senses—sight, hearing, smell, touch, and taste. Some had a sixth sense, which varied in form, from telepathy and clairvoyance to necromancy.

"Necromancy?" said C.J.

"I think that means the ability to communicate with the dead," Cille said.

Below the printed text was a handwritten note.

The Evadeam family shows evidence of the sixth sense.

Raine remembered what her aunt just said, *Or perhaps having the sixth sense.* "There is a list of names here." Raine noticed that the handwriting of the names varied in style and ink. "I don't think the same person wrote all these names."

Cille agreed. "Some look older, like they aged over time."

C.J. pointed at a scrawled-out name. "Cille, that's your name. *Lucille Evadeam.*"

"It could be the grandmother who I'm

named after," said Cille.

"But you have necro-whatever-you-call-it," reminded C.J.

"Guys, look who else is on this list." Raine placed her forefinger below the name *Adelaide Evadeam*. "Did you know our great aunt can see ghosts, too?"

"No," Cille replied.

"Me either."

"This book really is our family history," Raine stated.

"I think we need to be careful what we tell other people."

The three agreed. They were just about to put the book away when Uncle Greg walked back into the room to say good-night. "What book did you bring, C.J.?" Then his smile faded when he realized what they were holding. He quickly walked over and grabbed the book. "Where did you get this?"

His reaction surprised the kids. C.J. was quick to recover. "Aunt Adelaide gave it to us."

Uncle Greg paused and thumbed through it. "It should be locked away, not here."

"Why?" Raine asked "Aunt Adelaide said we need to read it. She says it's our family history."

"Dad, is this book magical?" C.J. was the most skeptical out of the three, but he couldn't deny

Cille's gift. He had witnessed it himself.

Uncle Greg struggled with the answer. "It's valuable and without the green stone—"

"This stone?" asked Raine. She held up her necklace that had a green stone on the key pendant.

"Aunt Adelaide gave that to you, too?"

Raine nodded. "We found something in the book. Can I show you?" She turned to the page with the scrawled names. "Is this Cille?"

Uncle Greg studied the name list. "It has grown."

"What has grown?" asked Cille.

"This list has changed since I read it last." He paused, "and the list appears when someone new is added."

"I knew it!" C.J. jumped up "it was your name Cille!"

"My name was added to the list?" Cille quietly asked.

Uncle Greg studied the names for a moment "It could be, but it is okay. It's nothing to be afraid of Cille. There is a lot of family names in here that you will recognize." He handed the book to Cille as he ran his free hand through his hair. "It's getting late and I'm tired. We have to get up early tomorrow. We can discuss the book more on the drive home. I should watch over the book, but…" He glanced at Raine's necklace, "but you have the protection necklace."

"Protection necklace?" questioned C.J.

"See, there is much you do not know. Aunt Adelaide should not have given you kids this book." He glanced at Raine, "it is safest near the green stone." Cille handed the book back to Raine. "Whatever you do, don't remove the necklace." Uncle Greg said sternly.

"Okay," replied Raine as she subconsciously touched the green stone. She now had more questions about the book and her family than ever before. But strangely, she did not feel scared — not too much anyway. She also did not feel so afraid of the ghost they had encountered earlier. *Did she have a sixth sense? Would she someday be in the book?* She was starting to understand what spiritual guidance meant. She made a mental note to ask Cille how she felt about being in *The Prophecies and Powers of Trahe* and how she dealt with poltergeists.

Puppy Jump

Raine awoke to the morning sounds of Uncle Greg moving around. At least they got to sleep until seven this time. After checking out of the hotel, they ate at a local diner for breakfast. Soon, they were on the same road they had driven the day before, except now they were heading east. They stopped at the Iowa 80 truck stop once more to fuel up and get some snacks.

As they were standing in line to pay, a gentleman in front of them was asking for directions to Erie, Illinois. The cashier politely told him to continue on I-80, then go north on 74 and east on 88. The man thanked him and left.

When the Evadeams left the store, Raine noticed the same man was sitting on a bench staring at a map. "Isn't that the same guy who was asking for directions, Uncle Greg? He looks confused."

"Seems that way to me, too." Uncle Greg walked over. "Do you need some help with directions?"

The man looked up. "I am supposed to be in Erie in an hour. But the guy in there said it will take me longer because of the snow."

"Tell you what," Greg replied, "I am driving that way anyway. Follow me and I'll take you to the right exit. You'll get there in time." He gestured at his truck. "That's my rig over there."

The man pointed at an old, rusted brown Pinto. "That's my car."

"I'll highlight your route on the map in case you lose me. But just keep following my truck, and you'll be good to go."

"Okay," agreed the man.

"I'm Greg, by the way."

"I'm Gabriel. It's very nice to meet you." He shook Greg's hand. "And thanks for your help."

"No problem."

As Uncle Greg and the children climbed into the cab, C.J. piped up. "Dad, isn't Erie off our route?"

"A little. We'll just take a small detour. We've got time."

As the truck rolled out of the parking lot, Raine thought about how kind his uncle was. They made it to the Erie exit within fifty minutes. Uncle

Greg pulled over, got out of the truck to make sure Gabriel could continue on his own. He reassured Greg he could and thanked him again.

Uncle Greg hopped back in the cab, but before he had a chance to take off, Gabriel was knocking on the window. Uncle Greg rolled it down. "I must tell you that it's okay to listen to the spirits. May the vision keepers guide you." He smiled warmly. "Okay. God bless. Thank you. Bye." And the man went off to his car.

No one said a word. Uncle Greg watched the Pinto drive away.

C.J. broke the silence. "Am I the only one who thought that was weird?"

Very weird. Only a few living on Earth knew of the Vision Keepers, Greg thought. He kept that to himself and instead said, "God sometimes works in mysterious ways."

Almost four hours later, they approached Michigan. Uncle Greg picked up the CB mic. "Hi, Eastbound I-94 truckers. This is Joker. Is the chicken coop at New Buffalo open?"

Affirmative, Joker. Yardstick two is open and crawling with full-grown Bears. Winter storm coming across the big lake.

Uncle Greg pushed the mic button. "Thank you." He returned the mic to its cradle. "Kids, we're going to stop at the next exit, which has a truck stop there. If we make it fast, we should be able to drop off my load in Grand Rapids before closing."

Cille watched as they exited the freeway for New Buffalo. She knew they were near Lake Michigan. She loved everything about the area—the beaches, the water, the quaint towns, and even the way they looked, covered in ice and snow.

"Will we have a chance to go to the lake?" Cille asked.

"Sorry, we won't have time. Plus, it's hard to maneuver the truck on the lakeshore roads."

Raine was a little thankful—she was ready to get home. The trip had been exciting, but they had been riding in a vehicle for a long time. She was ready to jump out as soon as they reached the truck stop.

Raine made a beeline for a basket of fruit at the coffee station. "I'm going to get a banana. Anyone else want one?"

"Yeah, sure," Cille said.

"No, thanks," said C.J. "Dad will start making us eat good food again as soon as we get home." He grabbed a bag of Doritos, red licorice, and a candy bar.

When Raine arrived at the coffee station, a small line had developed. A very old man was pouring his coffee. His hands shook so bad that coffee spilled over the counter and onto the floor.

"Dag nab it!"

Raine noticed that none of the adults watching offered to help the man. "Excuse me!" She moved to the head of the line. "I can help, sir. She grabbed a wad of napkins and cleaned up the spill. Then she poured the man coffee and asked what he would like in it.

"I take it black," said the man. "Thank you, young lady." He smiled.

"No problem. Why don't I help you carry it to the counter?" Raine grabbed the coffee cup and extra napkins. "Cille, grab me a banana please."

Cille took Raine's lead and cut in front of the adults who only complained about the wait while watching. "Excuse me," she said while grabbing their fruit.

The man insisted on paying for the girls' items.

"No, that's okay," Raine said. "We'll get it. Besides I'm not ready to check out yet. I forgot to get something to drink. Have a nice trip."

"Thank you for your kindness." The man grabbed Raine's hand and shook it. Then, he did the same for Cille. The girls watched the man as he walked outside into the snowy weather.

"Wow," Raine said.

"What?" asked Cille.

"Check out the man's car. *Fancy.*" The girls

watched the man get behind the wheel of a very expensive white Bentley.

Cille started to walk back to the coolers. "Come on. Let's get our drinks. Uncle Greg is waiting at the counter now."

Moments later they were pulling out and Cille noticed that the Bentley was still there. As the big rig started to roll, the old man's car slowly pulled out in front of them.

Her uncle stopped in time and waited for the vehicle to back out. "That was close."

"Maybe he shouldn't be driving," said Raine, remembering the man's shaky hands. The moment she said those words, the Bentley bumped into a small Civic. A fender bender.

A guy jumped out of the car that had been hit. He started yelling. Uncle Greg rolled down his window. The angry man was obviously uninjured. He was swearing. Then the guy pounded on the hood of the old man's car.

Uncle Greg jumped out of his cab. "Stay here, kids."

The girls moved to the front seats and watched with C.J. Uncle Greg went to the old man first to make sure he was all right. The kids watched as the gentleman assured Greg that he was fine. Then Greg approached the big guy cautiously. "Are you okay?"

The young man cursed and said, "This guy hit me!"

"I see that. It was an accident, and there is no reason to swear or hit his car. So you're fine?"

The guy went off on Uncle Greg, cursing even more. Then to get his point across, he hit the Bentley again.

Uncle Greg stood his ground. "I said no swearing and stop hitting the car." He pointed up to the cab. "I have kids in there." When the guy didn't back down, Uncle Greg lowered his voice "If you don't turn around and get into your own car, then I am going to take my rig, and 'accidently' smash into your car." He paused with a growl. "Got it?" Greg had no intention of smashing the Civic, but he got his point across.

The guy spared a look at the big rig. "Fine, but I am calling the police." He walked away.

As they waited for the police to arrive, Uncle Greg returned to the Bentley.

The old man climbed out of the car. "Thank you, I'm Richard Helldemueller. Please call me Richard."

"Helldemueller?" Uncle Greg said. "I have some relatives in Nashville, Michigan with that same last name."

"Oh, do you now? Maybe we are related."

"Maybe," replied Greg.

Just then, a bark came from the back seat. Uncle Greg saw a golden retriever puppy paw at the rear window. "And that is a lost puppy," explained the old man.

Cille had noticed the puppy too, peeking into the window.

"It's so cute!" exclaimed Cille. "I have to meet it." She opened the door.

"Cille!" yelled Raine. "Uncle Greg told us to stay in the truck." Cille was already out of the truck. Raine glanced back at C.J.

"Go ahead," C.J. said. "I'll watch the truck." He liked the idea of sitting behind the wheel.

Raine caught up with Cille and they ran to Uncle Greg. The gentleman was telling their uncle about the puppy. "I found the puppy in a rest area. Poor thing was hungry and alone. I didn't want to leave him. I was on my way to visit family. Thought they would want her, but they said no. I was just leaving their home and was trying to decide if I should keep her or drop her off at an animal shelter." He petted the puppy's head. "This little gal is the reason I hit that car. She barked suddenly and completely distracted me."

"Not a shelter," cried Cille, petting the puppy. "Wait a minute..." Cille petted the puppy. "Did you say you found her at a rest area?"

"Well, yes."

Uncle Greg bent down to the puppy "It can't be."

"It is! It has to be," exclaimed Cille.

Uncle Greg explained that they saw a puppy at a rest area yesterday but assumed he was with an owner.

"I bet it is the same one," agreed Raine.

"How old do you think she is?" asked Cille. She was thinking of that poor puppy being all alone during the snowstorm. Now, she really felt bad about leaving it yesterday.

"I am guessing a few months old," Richards replied. "Hard to tell because she has lost some weight from not eating." He hesitated and eyed Uncle Greg. "I don't suppose you are in need of a puppy?"

"Yes!" said Cille.

"No, Cille," Uncle Greg said quickly. "I don't think your parents would want it. You already have enough pets." He looked over at Raine. "But I bet I can talk *your* parents into it." He smiled.

"Me?" Raine would love a puppy. She had never had a pet, except for a fish in an aquarium. "My parents wouldn't want it either—Mom always says dogs are too much work, and Aunt Adelaide has a cat." She pushed her hands into her front pockets and resisted the temptation to pet the cute dog.

Her uncle grinned. "Cleo and Aunt Adelaide love dogs. And I know I can convince your parents."

What was her uncle up to?

"Are you sure we can have her?" Uncle Greg asked Richard.

Richard smiled. "Of course! I am pleased to see her go to a sweet young lady." He winked at Raine.

Richard gestured for Uncle Greg to grab the puppy and hand over to Raine.

"Thank you," said Raine.

"Raine, it is meant to be. Remember the picture in the book?" whispered Cille.

Raine nodded, but she was still afraid to fall in love with it. The puppy was so soft and cuddly though.

The cops arrived, followed by a black Cadillac Escalade. A man and woman jumped out of the SUV. "Dad," said the man anxiously. "Are you all right?"

"Oh, fuddle buckets!" said Richard. "Who called my son? One of his local cop buddies? I'm perfectly fine."

The woman gave Richard a hug. "What a relief."

The son immediately took his father aside. "Dad, you shouldn't be driving anymore at your age. You should use a chauffeur."

Uncle Greg turned to the girls. "Girls, let's give them some privacy. Go back to the truck. I have to give my witness report. I shouldn't be long."

The kids turned and walked slowly; it was hard to carry a five-pound puppy that was squirming and wanting to lick their faces. Cille couldn't wait to tell C.J. about the puppy miracle.

After Uncle Greg gave his eyewitness report, he went to say good-bye to Richard and his family. Richard Helldemueller shook Greg's hand. "Thank you for your help. You and your kids are angels."

"No, we're just human, trying to help when we can. We just happened to be at the right place at the right time."

"A sincere thank you," said Richard's son. "I appreciate you sticking up for my dad and watching over him until we arrived. If there is anything we can do in return, please don't hesitate to ask."

"You already have." He smiled. "We got a puppy."

Uncle Greg said his goodbyes and then hesitated. He whispered to the son, "Actually, there is something you could do for me. Are you serious about needing a chauffeur for your dad?"

"Yes, the police want to suspend his license. I think he'll have no choice, actually."

Uncle Greg explained how he had met the family at the truck stop. "The father could really use a job, and I am sure he would be willing to come back to Michigan for work."

"Sure, I can call him and check his qualifications."

Uncle Greg wrote the family's information on the back of a business card. "Thank you."

"No, thank you." He took the business card and gave Greg his own.

"God bless," Uncle Greg said before he walked away.

The old man silently watched the exchange and smiled as he leaned on his cane with light, soft snowflakes whirling around him.

Canine Cherub

Uncle Greg called Raine's mom, Alexander, and told her about the puppy. She was hesitate at first about keeping the animal, but after several cell phone calls — a final decision was made. Alexander cleared it with her husband, Scott, and Aunt Adelaide. She called her daughter's phone, and Raine screamed with delight when her mom told her she could keep the puppy.

Two hours later, the Evadeam family dropped off the truck load and began their way home. Raine's mom had told them to plan on eating dinner at their house. They arrived at the Helldemueller place well past supper time, starved. Aunt Adelaide and Raine's mom, Alexandria, welcomed them with open arms.

"Oh, isn't the puppy adorable," exclaimed the great aunt. The puppy wagged her tail and licked the aunt's face.

"She is cute," agreed Alexandria. "However, I think the puppy should stay in the mud room for now," she instructed. "I will get some dishes for his food and water."

Raine reached out for her mom's hand. "Mom, thanks for letting me keep her."

Alexandria smiled, bent down and kissed her daughter on the cheek. "Your welcome. Now, let's get you and this puppy some food."

When they entered the kitchen, they could smell honey-baked ham and chocolate chip cookies. Aunt Tricia, who had been watching Greg's three other boys, had arrived earlier that day to help prepare dinner for them. It was a great welcoming. C.J.'s brothers rushed to see the puppy and helped with the dog dishes while the four travelers collapsed in the kitchen chairs. They waited for their family to come in from the mud room, said a prayer and dove into the food.

"Thanks, aunties," said C.J. as he shoveled mashed potatoes into his mouth. "This tastes great!" C.J. paused when he heard the puppy whine. "Can he have some ham?"

"No, table scraps are not good for the dog," pointed out Uncle Greg.

"I went to the store and bought the dog some puppy chow," said Alexandria. "After your dad convinced me to keep the stray pup."

"So how did you end up with a puppy?" asked Aunt Tricia. Uncle Greg filled her in on their road trip adventures including the acquiring of the dog.

"Raine, what are you going to name your new puppy?" asked Aunt Adelaide.

"I don't know," after she chewed a piece of yummy ham. "We thought of some names on the way home — Golden, Sunny, Yellow. But I am not sure if I like any of them."

"How about Rover since we found her while traveling?" suggested Uncle Greg.

"The puppy is a girl," said Cille. "We can't name her Rover. How about Lost or Vanish since she was a lost puppy? Oh, wait! How about Angel since angels must have watched over her while she was abandoned at the rest area for so long?"

"Yeah, I can't believe she didn't die in that snowstorm," said C.J. as he scooped seconds onto his plate.

Alexandria's cell phone rang. She glanced at the number "It is your dad." She excused herself and stepped into the next room. A few minutes later, she called Raine over. "Dad wants to speak to you."

Raine ran to her mom and took the phone. "Hello?" As her mom walked back into the kitchen, she heard Uncle Greg asked if there was any word on their missing relatives. Her mom shook her head no.

Raine decided not to ask her dad about the investigation. They talked about the road trip instead. Then, he asked Raine "Have you come up with a name for the mutt yet?"

"Dad, she is not a mutt! She is a beautiful golden retriever." Raine was overjoyed and smiled. As she held the cell phone up to her ear, a painting on her aunt's wall caught her eye. It was one of her mom's favorite paintings of a guardian angel watching over a boy and a girl crossing a bridge. In fact, her mom had a smaller version of that same picture in her bedroom. *A guardian angel had to have taken care of her puppy.*

Raine thought she heard the puppy bark and a voice said cherub. She looked around seeing no one, but the thought had stuck. *Cherub! That's it!* "I will call her Cherub," she announced to her dad.

"I like that. It sounds fitting. Well, I will see you and Cherub in a couple of days. Love you, Raine."

"Love you, too … and Dad? Thanks for Cherub."

"You're welcome, baby. Good night."

"Night."

Raine felt happy—a happiness that she had

115

not felt in a long time. She bounced back to the kitchen table and handed the phone to her mom. She gave hugs to her great aunt and mom. "Thanks again for letting me keep the puppy."

Her mom squeezed her daughter "You're welcome. Now finish your dinner. We have fresh chocolate chip cookies for dessert."

Raine returned to her seat. "I'm naming her Cherub," she announced.

"Cherub?" C.J. wrinkled his face. "What kind of name is that?"

"I love it!" said Cille. "It's perfect."

The puppy barked in the back room. "See even she liked her new name," claimed Cille.

"She probably has to be let out," said Uncle Greg.

"Puppies are a lot of responsibility," said Aunt Adelaide. Aunt Tricia nodded her head in agreement.

Raine picked up her plate and set it in the sink. "I don't mind."

"Why don't you kids take the puppy outside while we clean up," Uncle Greg instructed.

As the kids and the puppy stepped out into the darkened and cool world, Raine looked up at the sky. It was filled with a full moon and twinkling stars. Her parents told her that Mother Earth and the above was created by something larger than themselves. Mom calls the powerful being God, but Raine noticed the Evadeam family say The Creator. Raine never gave it much thought until now. There were too many coincidences happening in her life this past year—heck, the past few months. Cherub barked. Raine looked down and then back up. "Thank you," she whispered to an invisible spirt above. She then wondered if the family magical book tied in with The Creator.

Clouds started to move in covering the bright stars. "I think the southern snow is coming our way," said C.J. Cherub started barking and ran to the back door to be let in. "I think Cherub knows it too."

The kids reluctantly followed her into the house. Uncle Greg announced it was time for the rest of them to head to their homes. They gave hugs and said goodbyes. Raine and her new puppy watched the truck roll out.

After she unpacked, Raine pulled out the book. She showed Aunt Adelaide the new pages that revealed the kids road trip adventures. "See, I told you the book was the answer," stated the great aunt.

"It is kind of freaking me out," admitted Raine. "And I'm not any closer to figuring out how to find our missing relatives."

"Hmm, maybe you are not supposed to help

them. Maybe you are supposed to help yourself with your own grand adventures."

Raine's mom walked in. "Hey baby. I found some old towels that we can use for Cherub's bed until we buy her a doggie pillow." She waved Raine over not even noticing the book "come help me. Plus, the dog needs to be let out again."

"Like I said, a puppy is a lot of work," laughed Aunt Adelaide. "I will do some reading while you work on your new chores."

"I don't mind. I have a new puppy!" Raine skipped away to her new friend.

After they left, Aunt Adelaide studied the page with the puppy drawing. Her aging hands then thumbed to the page revealing her brother. "Oh, Ovid, where are you? Are you back on the planet Trahe?" she whispered.

She touched the green stone on her necklace. The stone had powers. The children were starting to believe in the magic, but she knew the truth. The power of the stone comes from its source — Trahe. She knew in her heart, the Creator had plans for Raine. Plans currently unknown to herself. And the puppy — she didn't believe it was a coincidence that her beloved cat has disappeared and now another creature has arrived in her home.

What shall I do? Pray? Pray. She folded her hands and prayed for her missing family members including her cat, Cleo. She then prayed for her family here on Earth ending with a protection prayer for the book.

Christmas Essence

A week after their road trip ended, Raine was getting ready to attend Christmas Eve church service. Raine hadn't seen Cille or C.J. since they had been back, so she was excited about tonight. She would be able to see her cousins since many of the Evadeam family members attended on Christmas Eve. Raine's family got there early, so they could find enough rows of seats to accommodate all of them.

Her cousins arrived. "Hi guys," she said as they slid in next to her. C.J. leaned over and whispered, "Gideon is here with his mom. I didn't know his family attended our church."

"Maybe they just started." Cille said as she glanced around the sanctuary for Gideon.

Raine suddenly felt bad for him. She felt guilty for being mean to the boy at school. Her thoughts were interrupted by the sound of bells ringing through the church.

The Christmas program was starting. Raine sat through the service and enjoyed it. Besides scripture readings to remind everyone the true meaning of Christmas, they sang Raine's favorite traditional songs. The service ended with a candlelight vigil to the song of *Silent Night.*

Raine followed the family out into the lobby area where she ran into a girl named, Penny. She attended the same school and is the niece of the cop they saw on their road trip. He had mentioned joining a group at church.

"Hi, Raine," Penny said. "How was your holiday break?"

"Good."

"My uncle asked me to speak to you. I belong to a new small church group. We focus on anti-bullying. At school, we also have an anti-bullying campaign that involves student advocates. The advocates get special training so we can act as allies to those who are feeling scared, isolated, or mistreated. We thought that you would like to be an advocate. Interested?" Penny saw Raine's cousins approaching. "Maybe the Three Deams could join."

Raine remembered the man who needed help getting to Erie and how her Uncle Greg had assisted him. Then, there was the old man who they had helped at the gas station. What did Grandpa Ovid always say? *The Evadeam family was put on Earth to help those who cannot help themselves.*

"Why don't you sign me up and I'll talk to my cousins." Raine wanted to be a person who could help others ... without violence.

"Okay, I will. See you at school. See ya Cille and C.J.," said Penny as she headed back to her parents.

Raine explained the group to her cousins. They agreed it was a good idea. As they walked down the outside church steps, Raine left the church feeling proud. She also made a mental note to try to be nicer to Gideon in the future.

The following Saturday after Christmas, the downstairs of Raine's home was filled with Evadeam and Helldemueller relatives. They were hosting the annual family Christmas party.

Raine's mom and Aunt Adelaide were fabulous hostesses. They turned the old Victorian home into a winter wonderland with a real live pine tree placed in the front parlor. The Helldemueller House now resembled a place right out of *Better Homes and Garden* magazine. Her mom had even put a red velvet bow on Cherub.

Raine, Cille and C.J. filled small holiday plates with food. One of the family members owned a catering company, so the fare was displayed beautifully throughout the house. Raine thought it was incredible. After a while though, she needed a break from the overcrowded house. C.J. and Cille agreed, so they snuck upstairs with their refreshments and headed into Raine's room.

Cille giggled. "We made it. Your mom would kill us if she knew we were eating in here."

Raine laughed and put a plate on the floor for Cherub. "Yeah. Let's just try not to spill. Leave no evidence. Mom has been in a good mood, so I don't want to spoil it."

A few minutes later, someone knocked on the bedroom door. One of C.J.'s brothers stepped in. "Great Aunt Adelaide would like everyone to sing Christmas songs. Your mom said come down."

C.J. moaned. "We just got up here."

"Come on," encouraged Cille. "It will be fun. I love to sing Christmas songs."

As they descended the stairs, they heard the sound of the piano playing in the front parlor. It was Aunt Adelaide's favorite Christmas song, "Hark! The Herald Angels Sing," filling the house.

The Three Deams got a good view from the staircase. Aunt Adelaide was playing the piano beautifully. She looked upward and smiled as her gaze met Raine's.

As Raine smiled back, she realized how

happy she was. Her life had changed so much since she came to Nashville. She had dreaded going to big family gatherings before, but now Raine was actually enjoying it. She would have never imagined living in a big grand house with such an extraordinary great-aunt, or a road trip that had help cause such a change in her life.

Suddenly, Raine felt a chill and for a moment, she wondered if there was a ghost nearby. Cherub walked up to Raine and nuzzled her nose under the girl's hand. She pet her puppy and smiled. Raine pushed away the ghostly thought. This was not a time to be thinking about spooks.

As the party wound down, a latecomer showed up on the outside front doorstep. The three kids were sitting in the parlor. "You won't believe who's here," C.J. said as he peered out the window. "It looks like the old man who gave you Cherub."

The three kids watched as Aunt Adelaide welcomed the man into her home. "Richard, it has been a long time."

"Yes, it has. Your nephew, Greg, invited me. I hope that's okay."

"Of course, I am delighted to see you." She took her free hand and embraced his arm. "Seems we both have acquired a need for a walking cane."

"Yes, seems so."

The three kids was learning from Uncle Greg

that Richard Helldemueller was a distance cousin of Aunt Adelaide's deceased father-n-law. There was some family feud that had caused turmoil within the Helldemueller family long ago. "Amazing how Christmas can heal all things," he murmured.

"Agreed, young man," declared Richard as he walked into the parlor. "And I have more good news. Remember the family that you helped in Des Moines?" he asked. "Well, he was much too overqualified to drive my ole self around. But this is even better; my son called the gentleman in for a job interview. He got the job and was able to move his family back to Michigan. We also found temporarily housing through our church."

"How cool is that?" remarked C.J.

"*That* sounds like a miracle," declared Aunt Adelaide. "A real Christmas miracle." Or was it? As Cherub bounced into the room and put her furry golden paws on Richard, she wondered. *Was it possible that her lost feline friend or new canine pup had anything to do with the lives that had been changing recently?* She smiled and continued to enjoy her family and friends during her marvelous party.

Raine could not agree with her great-aunt more. Raine had witnessed many miracles. She thought about all she had accomplished in the past few months. Joined a mission to stand up against bullies and hopefully transform them in the process.

Helped a homeless family connect with someone who could assist them. Her great aunt now united with her long lost cousin. Raine had witness suffering and felt it herself. She had witnessed passion and now had passion herself: like the book and the puppy. And best of all — she has two best friends. *Life is good.*

Long after the sun had set and when the stars twinkled in the black sky, the Helldemueller house was quiet. Most of the guests had gone, except for those who decided to spend the night. Cille slept with Raine while C.J. slept in the guest room next door with his brothers. The girls buried themselves under Raine's purple and green comforter.

The sounds of a soft creak and a dog growling woke Raine. A chill filled the air. Raine opened her eyes and saw a ghostly figure standing over her bed. *She knew it. She had a weird feeling earlier.* She sucked in her breath and pulled the comforter up to her chin. The man looked like the picture of Great-uncle Helldemueller, Aunt Adelaide's deceased husband. He pointed to *The Prophecies and Powers of Trahe* book on Raine's nightstand and whispered one word. "*Believe.*"

Cherub's growl turned into a bark. Then, the ghost was gone.

If it wasn't for the sound of Cherub's bark,

126

Raine would have thought maybe she was dreaming. She pinched herself just to make sure. Nope. She reached over and held her puppy to quiet her. "It's okay, Cherub."

"Raine?" Cille had awakened and had also seen the spirit. "Did you see that too?"

Raine nodded.

"You can see spirits now?"

Raine didn't answer, but held Cherub tighter. Cherub was only a puppy, but little did Raine know that her dog had been born with a mission. *An assignment to guide and guard Raine Evadeam.* The dog's instinct was to protect her master — her friend.

Cherub started growling again. The puppy jumped off the bed and chased nothing—or something—out of Raine's room. Cherub stopped herself at Raine's door.

C.J. came into the room. "What's going on?"

Cille looked over at Raine. "I think Raine may have just seen her first ghost. I just saw something too."

Cherub stopped whining and pointed herself at the door. Her fur stood on end.

"I'm grabbing my sleeping bag and pillow," decided C.J. "Is it okay if I sleep in here with you two and the guard dog?"

"Yeah," Raine whispered. "But what about your brothers?"

"They are still sleeping and what they don't know won't hurt them." He nervously glanced back at the door. "Or will it?"

"No, I told you, ghosts are friendly. Spooky, but never really mean harm." Cille nudged Raine "But since when do ghosts talk to you?"

"This is my first."

"Freaking out?" asked C.J. who was relieved not to have the gift. He wasn't sure what to believe—friendly ghosts or not.

"Kind of," said Raine wrapping her arms around her knees. She was debating whether she should go tell one of the parents when Cherub ran to Raine's nightstand. The puppy jumped up and knocked down the book. Pages flipped to a drawing of the ghost Raine and Cille just saw. On the other side of the page, was a picture displaying a cat wearing a green stone on her collar.

"Look, it is similar to the one on your necklace," declared C.J.

"And the one on Aunt Adelaide's necklace," piped up Cille.

"And on Cleo's collar. I think this picture is Cleo," said Raine as she gently rubbed her necklace. Strangely, she wasn't too freaked out.

Cherub wagged her tail and then jumped back on the bed. Raine pet Cherub and felt even better —safer. But not well enough to go back to sleep. The kids decided not to wake any adults yet and were too tired to study the book. Raine placed it back on the nightstand and turned on the TV. "How about a movie?"

"Not a scary movie," said Cille.

Raine grabbed the remote. "Agreed. I'm thinking a Christmas comedy. "

As the wind howled outside, the Three Deams huddled together with Cherub and watched a holiday show. The puppy eyed the book knowing that an invisible ink was writing in *The Prophecies and Powers of Trahe*. A new name was forming under Lucille Evadeam. *Lorraine Evadeam.*

Cille noticed the puppy's attention towards the magical book. She took a deep breath, but couldn't relax. Part of her wanted to get an adult, but part of her didn't want to be cowardly. She decided to get up and dig out her journal instead. "I can't seem to focus on the movie. I need to relax. Maybe writing in my journal will help." As she began to write, Cherub plopped her furry head on Cille's legs. Cille looked into the dog's eyes and felt calm. She knew what needed to be written.

Raine sat up in her bed and leaned over her cousin to see what she was writing. Lorraine Evadeam smiled and gave Cille a gentle hug as she read her kin's words.

Tonight, my cousin Raine has learned she can see

ghosts, just like me. Great Uncle Helldemueller told us to "believe." I think he means we should believe in the book.

With our family, anything is possible, including the stories in The Prophecies and Powers of Trahe book. Now that I have another family member who sees what I see, I feel we are stronger.

I do believe, and I believe we have a calling. A mission to make discoveries in our family history and future. And maybe we'll learn something. Maybe the Three Deams will change the world.

I feel more is too come. Something exciting that will take us on another journey. Great quests which I will call The Evadeam Adventures.

GLOSSARY

Adelaide Evadeam Helldemueller: Sister of Ovid Evadeam. Married to Peter Helldemueller.

Alexandria Evadeam: Wife of Brandon Scott Evadeam. Mother of Raine Evadeam.

Brandon Scott Evadeam: Father of Raine. Son of Ovid Evadeam.

Cherub: A puppy. A guide. A messenger for the Creator.

Cleopatra: A cat. A guide. A messenger for the Creator. Also known as Cleo.

Coby Evadeam: Son of Ovid Evadeam. Father of Lucille Evadeam.

Coby James (C.J.) Evadeam: Eleven year old son of Gregory Evadeam. He has three brothers (ages five, seven, nine).

Gabriel: A lost traveler.

Gideon: A student attending Nashville Elementary School.

Gregory Evadeam: Son of Ovid Evadeam. Father of C.J. Evadeam.

Hachmoni: A messenger from the past.

Lorraine (Raine) Evadeam: Twelve year old daughter of Brandon Scott Evadeam and Alexandria Evadeam.

Lucille (Cille) Evadeam: Eleven year old daughter of Coby Evadeam.

Nashville: Town located in Michigan where Cille, C.J. and Raine Evadeam live.

Ovid Evadeam: The grandfather of Cille, C.J. and Raine Evadeam. Ovid's seven children are
Brandon Scott, Coby, Larry, Gregory, Ronald, Tricia, and Rhonda.

Penny: Anti-bully student advocate.

Peter Helldemueller: Deceased husband of Adelaide Evadeam Helldemueller.

Rhonda Evadeam: Daughter of Ovid Evadeam.

Ronald Evadeam: Son of Ovid Evadeam.

Richard Helldemueller II: Cousin of Adelaide Evadeam Helldemueller.

The Prophecies and Powers of Trahe: The Evadeam family history book that is thought to possess magical powers.

Tricia Evadeam: Daughter of Ovid Evadeam.

A NOTE FROM THE AUTHOR

I am excited to publish the first book of my new series — *The Evadeam Adventures*, a companion series to *The Trahe Chronicles*. Like Cille in this book, I am a proud survivor of epilepsy. I would often lay in bed, imagining a different world. These ideas have floated in my head for years through school, college, and multiple careers.

And as a reader, I love stories where the characters and plots spanned across multiple books. Now I am writing books of my own, and I'm so very happy to share them with you.

You might notice that many of my books mention my home state of Michigan where I grew up. I still live in the northern state with my husband, son, and remembrance of our cat, Cleo. Cleopatra was the inspiration of the messengers in my books. I do believe in a spirit world that guides us down our paths. Along the way, we take this guidance and help others. Some of the tales in this story are inspired by true, actual events that were told to me. I hope you enjoyed this book. I also encourage you to have many great adventures of your own!

Fans — thank you for your visits, conversations, and purchases. I am looking forward to "seeing" you again and I wish you happy reading of *The Three Deams*.

If you'd like to contact me or order any of my books, please visit www.dlprice.net or www.storytymerealm.com

D. L Price

A NOTE FROM THE ILLUSTRATOR

Jereco Price graduated from Comstock Park High School in Michigan prior to attending Ferris University. He graduated with a Bachelor's Degree in Digital Animation and Game Design. Jereco started his career by doing freelance website design and graphics work. He now works as a marketing manager for a large retail automotive company. He applies his talents by creating various forms of multimedia such as web sites, videos, magazine ads and other marketing materials. His passionate hobbies include multimedia design, boating, video games, reading and Batman! His home continues in Michigan where he resides with his lovely wife, cat and golden retriever puppy.

Made in the
USA
Lexington, KY